CALEDONIA

Amy Hoff

Erebus Society

First published in Great Britain in 2015
Erebus Society

Revised Edition

Copyright © Amy Hoff 2017
Original Editor: Bella Book
Editor of the Revised Edition: Constantin Vaughn
Cover & illustration copyright © Constantin Vaughn 2017

ISBN: 978-0-9933284-3-5

For Alasdair

TABLE OF CONTENTS

About the Author I
Prologue V

Chapter One 1
Chapter Two 9
Chapter Three 21
Chapter Four 29
Chapter Five 35
Chapter Six 53
Chapter Seven 61
Chapter Eight 73
Chapter Nine 81
Chapter Ten 91
Chapter Eleven 99
Chapter Twelve 111
Chapter Thirteen 117
Chapter Fourteen 133
Chapter Fifteen 149
Chapter Sixteen 161
Chapter Seventeen 167
Chapter Eighteen 173

Dylan's Glossary 183

About the Author

Amy Hoff spent years travelling across the United States, living out of cars and cheap motels. She was a weightlifter and street-fighter, collecting monster legends across the country. Eventually she left the USA and continued travelling around the world. She was educated in Scotland and specialised in Scottish history, literature, and folklore. She is now a folklorist and historian whose primary research interest is monsters. She has never owned more than what can fit into a backpack and a suitcase.

CALEDONIA

The word *faerie* was once synonymous with the word *monster*.

Prologue

Yesterday, Leah Bishop didn't believe in faeries.
That was yesterday.

***

"What the hell," she croaked, because *awake* was definitely not what she wanted to be. She looked at the empty whisky bottle near the bed and smiled at it like an old friend, before the hangover hit her. Then she would hate the bottle and all that it stood for. In her heart, she knew that she would be forgiving and all would be forgotten by the evening, when she'd fall back into its arms. She loved whisky. It loved her back. They were destined to be star-crossed.

She wondered why she was awake. Then, she heard it again. A knock on the door. Leah grumbled, willed herself out of bed, and walked across the floor in bare feet. She pushed her front door open.

There was a very good-looking man standing on her doorstep.

Hell yeah, thought Leah. She started to grin, and then belatedly realised she hadn't brushed her teeth.

"A message for you, miss," said the man, handing her a packet. "Sign here."

Leah did as she was told. The man bowed deeply, turned on his heel, and walked down her front drive. He turned left, and vanished behind a hedge.

She closed the door and padded to the kitchen to make tea. She yawned hugely, watching the milky water turn brown. After the tea had steeped, she carried the mug and the packet into the living room.

V

She ripped it open. Inside was a stack of paper, with a letter of invitation. CALEDONIA INTERPOL was written across the top, in bright silver professional-looking letters.

The message underneath read:

Dear Miss Bishop,

We have heard many positive things about your unique knowledge and considerable skills. We would like to invite you to work with us in Glasgow, at Caledonia Interpol. You would be given the title of Detective Inspector, and a generous pay rise. Enclosed are the forms and a manual to get you accustomed to your new life, should you take us up on our offer. Please do not hesitate to call me upon receiving this. We do hope you will decide to join us here in Glasgow.

Yours sincerely,
Chief Inspector, Ben A. Donner, Caledonia Interpol

There was a telephone number at the bottom. Leah sipped her tea. She looked around at the emptiness of her flat, and the silence closed in on her like a tomb. She picked up the telephone and dialled.

"Hello?" she asked. "May I speak to the Chief Inspector?"

***

Leah took the job.
She couldn't stay in the same city, not anymore.
Six months it had been.
Six months and counting.
That long?
It felt like yesterday.

***

VI

She walked out of her house for the last time, and looked out over the beauty of Edinburgh. The castle on the rock above Waverley train station. The Royal Mile, the countless tourists, the history, and the somewhat smug feeling that she was living in the most luxurious city in Scotland. She was leaving this beautiful place for the dark, gritty streets of working-class Glasgow. If Edinburgh was Scotland's Paris, then Glasgow was its Detroit. Detroit was cars, Glasgow was shipping, and both now existed in a disused, abandoned state, living off of the memories of better days.

Leah sighed. Nothing in Edinburgh spoke to her heart anymore. As she boarded the train to Glasgow, and the conductor came by for her ticket, she handed it over in quiet triumph. The train pulled out of the station, and she looked up at Castle Rock one last time. In departing, she felt nothing. Edinburgh was now a place of the past. She would not return.

June 12th, 21:54

Well, I guess I'm going back.

I was offered a position in Glasgow, at the station there. The pay is good, and it will mean a promotion. I wish that I'd been able to continue to work in my field, but the police work has been interesting enough, and it puts food on the table. I will miss Edinburgh, the dark alleys and the winding streets. Everything seems fashionable here.

Tonight, I walked alone in the dusk along one of the alleyways near the Scott monument. The streets were crowded with tourists, and the evening was lovely for having a glass of wine as sunset faded to darkness. However, I prefer Edinburgh in winter, on a weeknight. The city is quiet, and you can feel the years. Edinburgh is beautiful in the evening, when the snow dusts the pavements of the small alleyways, and candlelight flickers from the windowpanes of the pubs along the road.

Unfortunately, everything here is also a reminder. The place where we met on the university grounds... the theatre where I saw his play... the pub where he spilled his drink on me, and then asked me out... the small restaurant where he asked me to marry him. He was handsome, and funny; I liked the way I would

VIII

catch him looking at me, and he brought me roses.

Then the world turned upside down.

Adam and I split up a few months back, and the divorce was finalised today. He's living with the new girl now. It's funny how you think you know someone, and then you realise they've been a stranger all along. It's odd... the Glasgow offer came through on the same day as the divorce finalised. Seems like it was just in time.

Tonight, I stood in front of the restaurant where he asked me to marry him. I looked inside, at the couples laughing, and the small fireplace aglow even in the middle of summer – this is Scotland, after all. As the crowds passed me, and the people inside were wrapped in their own love and conversation, I took off his ring for the first time, and I placed it on the windowsill. I faded into the crowd, and out of the life of this ancient city.

I will miss Edinburgh, its artistic heart, its Victorian charm that reminds me of Jekyll and Hyde, and the university where I learned about folklore... the stories of countless generations.

I still miss him... and his eyes, and his smile.

I need to get out of this city.

-Leah Bishop

Chapter One

The phone rang. Even in her sleep, even after all this time, she still hoped it was him. It never was.

Leah woke up with the taste of *day-after-whisky* on her tongue. She was confused for a moment, trying to orient herself as she sat up on the edge of the bed. She saw the half-empty bottle on the floor, next to a shortbread tin she had purchased in a fit of madness during the night. She stared at the castle and loch depicted on the lid, tiny Highland cattle dotting the landscape, and shook her head at the Scotland she had never known. Her Scotland was bookies and rundown neighbourhoods, drug addiction and poverty, loud clubs and council flats; a derelict fantasy of cheap booze, bad cigarettes, and terrible decisions.

The hotel was nothing to speak of. It was a humble affair, a compact white building at the centre of a row of houses. The cracked walls and cramped, hard bed served as a reminder of the city she was in. The bathroom, where the shower ran too cold or too hot, and the general cold damp of the building made her miss Edinburgh, and her small bright flat. When she had arrived in the city the night before, her new boss had spoken to her on the telephone, informing her that they were in the middle of a murder investigation. He'd explained that this was one reason they had recruited her.

Leah opened the blinds and stared blearily out at the grey nothing, rain dripping from the red sandstone of the run-down building across the alley.

"Right," Leah said aloud to her empty hotel room. "Glasgow."

The phone continued to ring. She sighed, then dug under the pillows until she found it.

"Hello," she croaked.

"Are you awake?" asked a male voice.

"I am now."

"You'll have to get down here as quickly as you can. There's something I need to show you."

Leah rolled her tongue around in her mouth, to see if that improved things a bit. It didn't. Grumbling, she sat up.

"Be right down," she said. After a shower.

Leah sat at the edge of her cold, hard bed, and stared at the carpet. She told herself police officers aren't supposed to cry.

***

Leah walked out of the underground station, haunted by her impending hangover. She'd been told that someone would be there to meet her, but the station seemed abandoned. She started to wonder if she'd gotten the time wrong, and checked her watch. 9 AM, St. Enoch Station. That was right, wasn't it? She heard the sound of footsteps behind her, and turned around.

The man standing there was impossible and beautiful.

He was slim, with black hair, and huge mournful eyes in a pale face. He was dressed in a tailcoat, pressed trousers, and gloves. His long, royal blue brocade tailcoat complemented the white of his skin. Leah's mouth dropped open, eyes wide in undisguised appreciation and utter disbelief. She wondered how much she had to drink the night before, and blinked.

The apparition remained, and held out a gloved hand.

"Leah Bishop?" asked the man. Leah was impressed. His cheekbones could slice apples.

"Yeah...?" she said.

The man bowed over her hand, and then kissed it. Leah continued to stare.

"I am Detective Inspector Dorian Grey," he said.

She knew that all detectives were plainclothes officers, but she wondered why he looked like someone from a steampunk convention. Even that wasn't quite accurate, though. This man

2

had an air of displaced reality, as if he had been removed from the Victorian era and placed on a kerb outside of St. Enoch Station at 9 in the morning. His huge eyes watched her, his face impossibly sad. Leah was reminded suddenly of a childhood pet: the way her black Labrador used to look up at her with his chin resting on her knee. She then realised what he had said.

"Dorian Grey?" she asked. "Did you make that up yourself?"

"Yes," said the man, without a trace of irony. He stood there staring, as if he were waiting for some kind of prompt.

"Er... on the phone you said you had something to show me?" she suggested.

"Indeed," he said. "We'd better go. The chief does not like to be kept waiting, and you know how difficult he can be, given his history."

"I do?" asked Leah.

"I'd assume so, yes," said Dorian. "Come along."

Leah hesitated, having never been told to 'come along' before. If this was her new partner she supposed she would have to get used to his idiosyncrasies. God knew she had enough of her own.

There was a large open square between the two entrances to the underground station, and in the centre of it was a strange building that resembled a castle. Two of its four turrets framed a large clock. The building now housed a coffee shop, and its many windows advertised the specials of the day.

"This used to be the subway station," Dorian explained, leading her around the back of the building. He stood in front of a solid brick wall, focusing on it. He took off a white glove, and pressed his bare palm to the red sandstone. Leah stared at him. Suddenly there was a strange sound, the ancient creaking of stone moving on stone, and a tunnel appeared; a tunnel of leaves and plants that descended into the darkness.

Leah turned to look at him very slowly.

"What the shit?" she asked.

Dorian bowed.

"After you," he said.

"I am not still drunk enough for this," muttered Leah. She stared down into the darkness. *It's this, or back to Edinburgh.* And the memories. She took a deep breath.

Leah cautiously took the first step down the stairs. Dorian followed her, and as they descended, she heard the door slowly close. Around them, a phosphorescent light illuminated the staircase and the leaves, giving the impression of a moonlit garden. Uncomfortable with the strange silence, and the general situation, Leah spoke.

"So... does the chief let you dress like that?" she asked.

The eyes of small creatures watched her, bright and black, from behind the leaves. Slight whispering and tittering made her whip around and nearly lose her balance on the stairs. She caught the railing just in time, her head starting to ache.

Dorian looked down at his impeccable clothing, apparently not noticing Leah's discomfiture.

"Like what?" he asked.

"Like..." she began, indicating his outfit and then thinking better of it, "er... never mind."

He raised an eyebrow without comment, as they continued down the staircase.

"As I was saying earlier," he said, "we called you in because of your unique knowledge and skills."

"So you said," she replied, and wondered what kind of skills she had that would be valuable.

"My what now?" Leah's mind helpfully supplied Adam's words, telling her repeatedly that her knowledge was worthless. She sighed. How had she fallen in love with someone like that?

"That would be Adam, I take it?" asked Dorian, as if she had spoken aloud.

Stopping dead, she looked into the wide brown eyes of the strange young man.

"How do you know about him?" she demanded.

He shrugged slightly.

"I can hear it in your heartbeat," he said, pausing on the staircase. "Are you coming?"

4

Now, she was even less certain about the wisdom of following Dorian, as they continued to descend into the darkness. She watched him: perfect posture, delicate bone structure, like something she had seen in a film, or a painting. He reminded her of wilderness and of the sea, of forest creatures at the close of day, of faithful pets. As if he weren't quite human.

They finally stepped down from the staircase onto a long, winding path overhung with an archway covered in ivy and flowers. It was beautiful, and tiny white lights showed the way as the small creatures living in the plants continued to chirp and whirr at them as they walked.

Leah was entranced. It was the kind of magical place she'd imagined as a child.

"The reason that we called for you," Dorian said, startling her, "is because we think a human is killing them."

"Them who?" asked Leah.

"Perhaps I should say us," he said. "Killing... *us*."

Suddenly, they had reached the end of the pathway. Dorian took out a large silver skeleton key with a heart-shaped Celtic knot on one end. He inserted it into the lock, turned it twice to the right and once to the left. He lifted the huge wrought-iron hoop and the ancient wooden door swung open. Leah looked around herself, and was a bit deflated to see that they were in what appeared to be a broom closet.

"Is this a cupboard?" she asked. Dorian looked at her.

"We've had some... budget cuts," he said.

***

As he led her down what looked like a normal hallway, her mind was racing. *What is happening? Have I been drugged? Probably not, maybe this is what the world is like when you're sober, Bishop. Do you even remember what that's like? There's no way... is this real? There is no way this could possibly be real...Is there? Is this magic?*

At the end of the hallway, Dorian knocked on a white door.

The door swung open, and Leah drew a breath. They stood in a Jacobean library, filled with light and life. The room was packed full of books with overstuffed red sofas lining the walls. The room was huge, and the ceiling was so high... *was that a cloud?* that it had its own weather. Several walls were made up only of bookshelves stacked so tall it was difficult to see them in their entirety. Black wrought-iron spiral staircases stretched out of sight along the shelves. The carpets were red, the walls a tasteful combination of oak paneling and rich cherry mahogany. The three-dimensional latticed windows were large and arched, letting in the silver Glasgow sunlight. Outside the window was a large garden that did not look as if it belonged anywhere on Earth. There was an enormous fireplace in the centre of one wall where a large fire crackled merrily.

Leah was in love.

Small people - with *wings*? - were deep in conversation beside a teakettle, and various other people of all sizes and descriptions read over each other's shoulders and lounged on the sofas, or in the armchairs. Near each one of them, a small laptop computer whirred quietly.

In the corner, behind piles and piles of paperwork, seated in front of a desktop computer from the nineteen-eighties with a green-text monochrome monitor, was a giant. The giant looked up over his half-moon glasses, caught sight of Dorian, grumbled to himself, and went back to poking at the keyboard with a single fingertip.

Dorian smiled slightly.

"Who's that?" whispered Leah.

"Your new employer," Dorian replied, as the giant raised his ponderous bulk to come out from behind the desk. He towered over both of them.

"Welcome to Glasgow, Detective Inspector Bishop," rumbled the giant. "My name is Benandonner. I am the chief of police here."

Leah stared up at him, open-mouthed. Although he was taller and larger than Leah or Dorian, he merely looked like an oversized human to her.

Leah shook his hand, and then looked at both of them.

"Benandonner?" she asked. "Like the giant?"

"No, Leah," said Dorian. "He *is* the giant."

The world fell silent as she considered this. Benandonner and Dorian watched her placidly, waiting for her response.

"You expect me to believe that?" she asked.

"Are there magical portals in your world?" Dorian returned, and shrugged. "People were just shorter back then. He truly is the giant who fought Cuchulainn."

"And who are you? Cuchulainn?" Leah retorted. As far as she was aware, Benandonner was the giant who destroyed the Giant's Causeway to Ireland, for fear of Finn MacCool.

"Don't be ridiculous," he said. "I am the selkie Dorian Grey. And I *did* make it up myself. Humans cannot pronounce my real name."

Chief Ben cut in, exasperated, "Can we get down to business?" Dorian nodded.

"We think we're dealing with a serial killer," Chief Ben said to Leah, turning to her. "The first in our world. That's why we needed you, Leah - a human. You might find your qualifications in folklore useful in this position."

"And you've never had to deal with humans before?" Leah asked, thinking, *Am I really having this conversation? Are these people insane? Am I? I've never heard anyone call a Master's in folklore **useful** before.*

"No," he said, as if this was the strangest question she could have asked. "Do you think the human police have time to investigate supernatural crime? We're too busy policing ourselves."

"Policing yourselves?" asked Leah. "How do you mean?"

"Monsters have killed humans since they came into existence, all over the world," said Dorian.

"Humans were viewed as having been created as prey for the faerie people," said Chief Ben. "Interpol was founded centuries ago by monsters around the world that believed in the possibility of a peaceful coexistence. Something had to be done."

"Some of us even went to war over it," said Dorian, and there was an edge to his voice that suggested he was one of them.

"Say that I do believe you," said Leah, "Why would monsters still be an issue today? It's been centuries."

"The reason you never hear about it anymore is because this police force exists," said Dorian. "The monsters keep the monsters at bay."

"Okay, but why here?" asked Leah. "Why the city, instead of the Highlands?"

Dorian and Ben exchanged glances.

"This is Glasgow," said Chief Ben. "Even the faeries have drug problems."

Leah considered this information. She didn't exactly believe what they were telling her, but it still sounded better than the alternative.

"Well," said Leah, "I don't know how much help I can be, but... I'm game."

Especially, she thought, *if you lot are going to pay me. You can call yourself whatever you want, just pay me a lot of money and keep me out of Edinburgh.*

"Good to hear," said Chief Ben. "Welcome to the force. Dorian, can you show her the evidence? I have work to catch up on."

Turning away, the older man grumbled to himself, as he maneuvered around his desk to hide again behind the giant stacks of paperwork. It appeared that the interview was over, and Dorian indicated to Leah that they should go. He bowed slightly towards the stacks of paper, and crossed the room to another door.

Leah, still wondering about the wisdom of her choices, followed Dorian out of the Jacobean library that served as the base of operations for Caledonia Interpol.

Chapter Two

Leah followed Dorian through the door, and the room could not have been more different. It was so normal as to feel oddly out of place. The white walls and blue carpet were functional and sterile. The room was dominated by a large glass wall with photographs. Lines had been drawn from one to the next, with notes written hastily in English, Gaelic, and what almost looked like a mixture of cuneiform and hieroglyphs. She stepped closer. It was Ogham. Pictish Ogham. Not even scholars knew Pictish, or what the symbols represented; they could only guess. She turned to look at Dorian, who was already writing on the glass next to one of the pictures.

In Pictish Ogham, not English, or even Gaelic.

A part of Leah that had long been silenced was growing louder in excitement and wonder.

What if this is real? That would be more important than pay. Well, she amended, *almost.*

Leah walked up to the board and examined the photos of the victims. The killings appeared to have been bloodless. Each face stared at her blankly, and she tried to read the life in their eyes, to conceive of lives lived and now lost. It was difficult.

"They found the fifth body this morning," he told Leah, indicating the photographs. "Every one of them the same."

Dorian, while beautiful, had a sinister look to him. His permanently dour expression and the angles of his face and body gave him a sharp and menacing aspect. His huge, sad brown eyes, mournful expressions and some of his behaviours, like the way he moved his body, turned his head, and looked at people, reminded Leah more and more strongly of the pet Labrador of her childhood.

She leaned forward to look at the photos and instantly recognised several species of Fae from descriptions and woodcarvings. Leah went into research mode, hangover forgotten, as the folklorist she had been at university. She felt wonder and deep grief as she looked at the creatures she had spent her entire life studying. There was a glaistig, lying on her side, eyes glassy. A joint-halver, its small, troll-like body limp and splayed across the pavement. They lay there with peaceful looks on their faces. The only image in which damage had been done was of a faerie with broken wings. There was, however, a pattern.

"We don't know what killed them," Dorian said. "The Fae are notoriously difficult to kill. Yet, many of the creatures here were very powerful beings. And all of them are dead. We just don't know how."

Leah leaned in to look closely at one of the photographs. There was a message above the corpse, scrawled out in black spray paint.

"*Murdering Reality,*" Leah read aloud. She turned to Dorian. "What does it mean?"

Dorian held her gaze. It was unnerving, as if she was staring directly into history.

"It s an old term, meaning death to humans," said Dorian. "There are some of us who don't take kindly to them."

"You're right," she said softly. "I think it is a serial killer."

A breath, soft and gentle, stole across the room and brushed Leah's cheek. She heard it, an audible sigh. Quiet strains of ethereal music wafted through the air and settled around her.

She turned as she heard the door open, and in walked the most handsome man she had ever seen. His large brown eyes were soft. He looked exotic and flawless, his complexion dark, and when he shook out his long hair, chestnut curls tumbled over his shoulder. His soft, insinuating smile reminded her of clean bedsheets and candlelight. Leah did not realise she had been staring. Dorian turned to look at the newcomer and rolled his eyes.

"Turn that down, would you?" said Dorian. "It's ungodly."

"Sorry," said the young man, turning his charm directly towards Leah. "Detective Inspector Magnus Grey."

"Leah Bishop," she stuttered. "Wait. Did you say Grey?"

He shook her hand, and Leah felt the spell draining away, as if someone had indeed turned down the intensity. She missed it as soon as it was gone.

"Yes," said Magnus, gesturing towards Dorian. "We're...*brothers*."

"Indeed," said Dorian witheringly. "Honestly, Magnus, there's no need to walk around with it... what do they say these days? *Turned up to eleven*."

"Well," said Magnus, grinning rakishly at Leah, "The ladies seem to like it."

"I'm sure they do," said Dorian, with as much hauteur as he could muster. "Now, is there anything *important* you would like to discuss?"

"Oh, yes," Magnus replied. "The murderer knows about Interpol. We received a message here at the station, the same *Murdering Reality* phrase. It was hand-delivered, and left on Ben's desk. There's more at stake here than the Fae dying. The killer seems to have infiltrated the station. I think we might need to speak to our informant."

Dorian nodded.

"Agreed," he said. "Let's go."

***

Leah followed the two selkie brothers through the interlinked alleyways of the city. Whenever the light changed, shadows played across their features, and she was so strongly reminded of seals that she had to blink occasionally in order to view them as men.

Glasgow was dark, and tinged red, with a fine coating of grit. The streets were winding, but functional. This was a city of manual labour, coal, and tears. Leah could sense the sorrow and the darkness, as if it had seeped into the very stones. Sometimes it could be beautiful, she thought, in its unrelenting hardness.

The three of them stepped into a close situated between two red brick buildings, cool in the afternoon damp. The sounds of traffic could be heard in the distance, but otherwise, it was cut off and private. Leah halted on the staircase.

"All right, stop," she said.

The two seal-men turned to her, and she saw their eyes glow faintly in the dark. A deep dread suffused her entire being, and a strange vision momentarily washed over her.

Seals, on a dark Highland beach as the moon comes out, lifting their heads and watching with glass-black eyes as waves crash against the shoreline.

She stared for a moment, the sudden and unexpected fear fading as quickly as it had arrived, and then spoke again.

"This is a lot to take in," she explained. "I have to know - why me? What can I possibly offer in this situation?"

"Someone has been killing off supernatural creatures, one by one," said Dorian. "There's no rhyme or reason to it. The victims have been of every alignment - good, bad, and neutral. There seems to be no pattern."

"We think the killer might be human," said Magnus.

Leah shook her head in frustration.

"Yes, but *why*?" she asked. "What is it about these murders that make you think it couldn't be a - a supernatural?"

"Serial killing," said Dorian. "It is a human behaviour. Faeries just don't do that kind of thing. They'll kill, in war or for rage or vengeance, but there is no method. They aren't *killers*."

"We're monsters," agreed Magnus, "but we're not *monsters*."

"You think I can help because serial killing is *human*?" she asked. "I know nothing about serial killers. I'm not sure I can help simply because I'm human too."

"It is more than that," said Dorian. "We needed a human who knows about folklore. Someone who will be able to make connections that we cannot."

"And someone who is new to all this," said Magnus. "Someone with fresh insight. We've been doing this for... a *very long time.*"

Leah sighed, and looked upwards, where clouds moved across a pale blue sky.

"The note is a new lead, which is why we're going to speak to one of our informants," said Dorian.

"Great. Let's go talk to them," Leah moved to leave the close.

"We have to wait until nightfall."

"Why?"

"First," Dorian said, "we eat."

***

The café was sweet and quaint, its chairs and tables carved from wood but in keeping with the form of the trees from which they had been cut. It had a warm and jovial atmosphere.

Leah sat with Magnus and Dorian, who had already spent too long poring over the menu. When the waiter showed up, the two selkies looked at each other.

"Fish?" they both suggested. They both nodded. "Yes, I think fish."

"We'd like Loch Fyne oysters as a starter, pan friend salmon as the main, and - shall we order dessert now or later?" asked Magnus.

"Later is fine, sir," said the waiter. The men nodded, handing over their menus.

"And for you, miss?" he asked.

"Eggs Benedict and Bruichladdich, neat," Leah said, "and er, tea, with tablet, and a glass of water."

The waiter nodded, and left. Leah was staring at the brothers. Eventually Magnus noticed.

"What is it?" he asked.

"Did you both just order oysters and fish?" she asked.

"Yes," said Dorian. "I'm glad he's giving us time because I can't decide between caviar and smoked trout mousse for dessert."

Leah started to feel a bit ill.

"What about chocolate?!" she asked, "or cheese, or I don't know, cake?"

Dorian and Magnus looked disgusted and a bit horrified.

"You're not supposed to feed chocolate to animals!" said Magnus.

The selkies stared at her across the table with their huge dark eyes. For a fleeting moment, it reminded her of horror films where eldritch things watched from the shadows, strange and ancient. She shivered, and the feeling was gone. But not forgotten.

"Aren't you going to get anything to drink?" she asked. Magnus looked at her, puzzled.

"No," he said. "We get all the hydration we need from the food we eat."

"Do you always order the fish?" she asked. Dorian looked at her as if this was the most ridiculous question anyone had ever asked.

"Of course, Leah," he said. "We're seals."

The waiter showed up with a tray full of food. Leah looked at the wonderful meal spread before her with contented joy. Especially the whisky. She wrapped her hands around the mug of tea first.

"Did you hear that?" Dorian suddenly asked Magnus.

There was a ticking, clicking noise, and Leah thought that was what Dorian meant. Startled, she realised it was coming from them. They seemed to be communicating in some other, wilder language. The ticking became more pronounced, and then the two brothers stared forward, slowly tilting their heads at the same time. Through her, as though she wasn't even there. Their heads swivelled slowly to the right, and then tilted again. It was like a slow, dream-horror windup music box. Dorian turned to look at her suddenly and she nearly dropped her tea.

"Let's go," he said. "She's just opened the restaurant."

"And you know this... how?" asked Leah.

Magnus turned to look at her then.

"We can hear it," he said. "Seals have excellent hearing."

Leah thought of Dorian's mind-reading capabilities.

"I can't read your mind," said Dorian. "Only your heart."

"Should have guessed," she said. She set down her tea with a sigh, knocked back the whisky, pocketed the tablet, and left the table.

***

They walked through the grim twilight of Glasgow. The city's aesthetic didn't improve in the evening, although it always looked good through the lens of a whisky glass. It was a desperate city, with people who didn't know where to look or in what direction to turn. They certainly knew about alcohol, although they didn't seem to know what to do with it once they had it. It seemed as though drinking was temporary; nobody drank in Glasgow, alcohol just paid their stomach a holiday visit, in and out again. As they walked, Leah noticed that Dorian and Magnus shone in the night, like lamps. Dorian's skin was a silver colour, while Magnus's was gold. They seemed to absorb and reflect the night around them.

"Chief's calling me," said Magnus, looking at his phone.

"Go ahead," said Dorian. "We can take care of this."

Magnus nodded, and continued down the alleyway, turning left toward Buchanan Street to head towards St. Enoch.

"Wish we could go back with him," grumbled Leah, rubbing her arms in the chill damp of the evening and thinking of the warmth at Caledonia. She pictured herself there, with a cup of hot tea, doing research in the large library. Dorian nodded in agreement, and led her down an alleyway. His skin began to shine even brighter. It reminded her of pictures she had seen of phosphorescent creatures in the ocean at night.

"What's that?" asked Leah, pointing at the sheen.

"Moonlight," Dorian said, with a straight face. She stared at him.

"Seriously?"

He didn't reply, just turned a corner and went into a dark alley. The faint illumination he gave off was helpful, as it was black as pitch in there. A rectangle of light threw gold into the alleyway.

The beautiful selkie turned, the golden light of the restaurant playing off his cheekbones.

"Welcome to Desdemona's," said Dorian.

He gestured toward the doorway with one perfect white hand, and Leah walked through the door into another world.

She breathed in the warm smoke, a shisha haze that cast the warm, low light of the restaurant into a dreamlike wonderland. Rich tapestries hung from the walls, and the floor was littered with red pillows and intricate rugs. The sweet scent of tobacco mingled with spices that made her mouth water, as waiters carried plates of steaming food to the various tables. Dancers moved sinuously between the tables, as if they had been poured out of a jar, somehow avoiding the waiters and patrons. They seemed as though they were a part of the music, rather than just dancing to it; as if the music breathed life into their bodies, and they might vanish at the end of the song, ghosts of another time fading into a dream. To Leah, it felt very exotic, like the entrance to Faerie.

"No," said Dorian. "The entrance to Faerie is not here."

Leah rounded on him.

"Will you stop doing that?!" she asked, exasperated. Dorian shrugged.

"I can't help it," he said. "It's as loud as if you were talking."

"Can you tell the difference?" she asked.

"Yes?" said Dorian, puzzled.

"Then keep it to yourself!" she said. "If I want your participation, I'll ask."

Dorian bowed slightly.

"My apologies," he said.

Leah sighed, feathers settling.

"So, who are we here to see?" she asked. Dorian sat down at a nearby table and indicated one of the dancers.

❀ CHAPTER TWO ❀

"Her," he said.

She was tall, and extraordinarily fierce-looking. Her long hair was a shocking ginger colour against skin so white it was almost translucent. Her red lips were an exclamation in the centre of her face, and her green eyes seemed to burn like embers beneath long black lashes. She was not beautiful. She was intense. She was also a very skilled dancer. Leah wondered if it was difficult to learn such intricate movements.

Dorian called the waiter over, and he ordered some food in a language Leah did not recognise. A woman accidentally brushed up against him, and then apologised a bit too freely with her hands. Leah surreptitiously scanned the room, and saw that every woman - and a few men - were either staring at Dorian, blushing, or trying very hard not to look at him. The only person who wasn't doing any of this was the woman they had come here to see.

"Wow," said Leah, after the waiter had left. "I didn't realise I was sitting with a celebrity."

"Mmm?" asked Dorian, and then looked around himself. "Oh yes, that. The selkie curse."

"Doesn't look like much of a curse to me."

"You'd be surprised."

Leah noticed how people stared at him, came close to him, made up any excuse to touch him. He didn't seem to pay any attention, and that was the strangest thing of all. The set finished, and Dorian rose from the table, gesturing to Leah. She stood up and followed him outside into a small courtyard. The woman with the ginger hair was already there, lighting a cigarette. She turned, and saw Dorian. She sighed, clearly not welcoming the company.

"So. Murders," she said, and Leah was surprised to hear an American accent, "I can't say I care. I'm a murderer myself."

She inhaled deeply, the smoke curling from her lips as she breathed out, her bright green eyes hooded. She smiled, slowly. Leah got the sudden, overwhelming impression that she was baiting Dorian.

17

"Yes, thank you, Desdemona," said Dorian irritably. "We are aware that you are a vampire. You don't need to go to all that effort."

"Neither do you," she said. "What do you want to know?"

"You know things about this city, more than any of us do. Want to tell us if you've heard anything?"

She shook out her hair, and made a noise of unwilling cooperation. Dorian folded his arms. She put her red lips around her cigarette and inhaled slowly, enjoying Dorian's impatience.

"Not much. I just know someone's angry but I'm still not sure why. Nobody trusts a vampire. You certainly don't trust me."

"Our kind does not trust yours, for obvious reasons," he replied. He stood there staring for a moment, and seemed to lose some inner battle.

"Will you keep us posted if you do hear anything?" he finally asked.

"Anything you want, gorgeous," she bit out, flicking the butt of her cigarette into the street. She walked back into the restaurant and slammed the door.

"That went well," observed Leah.

***

Leah walked home, if a hotel could be called home. She mulled over what she knew, again and again, in her mind. Why use a phrase like *Murdering Reality*, an anti-human slogan, if the killer was human? From what she understood of folklore, faeries were incredibly resilient, if not immortal.

How could a mere human kill them?

She walked along Kelvinbridge on the Great Western Road, breathing in the city and considering various aspects of the case. She wondered how the killer would be able to access Caledonia, given the difficulty of doing so without magic. This meant that someone within the station was probably at fault, or was somehow related to the killer. She paused underneath one of the sodium lamps that served as the streetlights of the city, their orange glow giving the impression that Glasgow was on fire. Leah suddenly realised she was merely thinking like a police officer about a case, rather than the fact that she had just learned that Faerie was a real place, and that the various monsters she had spent her life daydreaming about were as real and solid as the bridge beneath her feet.

The air was cool and brisk, and a light mist settled against her skin. She stopped to look down into the dark water of the river. She needed to brush up on her monster lore. And she needed a strong glass of whisky. Maybe a bottle.

Definitely a bottle.

Chapter Three

eah opened one eye and surveyed the land beyond her pillow. She had the vague sense of a residual hangover, and that something very strange had happened. She swung her legs over the side of the bed, yawning. Suddenly she started. It hadn't been a dream. She was a detective now working for the monsters of Glasgow. There weren't a lot of things that could make a difference to her at the moment, but *faeries are real* has a way of burning through the worst hangover. She made herself tea, and sat down to stare at the wall for a good ten minutes. She caught her reflection in the mirror, and the scar that swept back from her right eye towards her hairline. She thought of the pains she had taken all her life to hide it. She thought of how it had happened, back in her childhood; how no one had believed her, and eventually convinced her she'd imagined it all. It had led to her ultimately pursuing a career in folklore.

Leah thought back on what had happened the day before, and smiled. Outside the window, children were playing, shouting and chasing each other in the rain. She realised she had been smiling since she woke up. The feeling was unfamiliar, but welcome, like the sun coming out over Scotland.

Leah drank down the remains of her tea and set the cup back into the saucer. She started the kettle boiling again. This must be what it felt like to have dreams come true. Had she been aware that there was a career path of 'faerie police officer' she would have signed up years ago. She could think of several other scholars who would have done the same.

As she poured her second cup of tea, she began to have misgivings. If this was real, what about her future? She had made a lot of choices in the past that hadn't guaranteed anything resembling stability, which was one reason she had lost Adam. She wondered now: was it time to be smart?

All her life, she could see two paths before her, one dark and uncertain, and another where she lived a common life, with security and stability, and she got a watch at the end. She sighed, as she drank her tea, and shook her head.

"No," she said aloud to herself. "I want more than a watch. I always have."

There was a knock on the door.

Leah crossed the small hotel room and opened the door.

Standing there, in his Victorian splendour, was Dorian Grey. He smiled and offered his arm.

"Care to join me, Miss Bishop?" he asked.

The door closed, and steam rose from the cup of tea, forgotten on the countertop.

***

They went to a local pub for the last hours of serving. Leah sat across from Dorian at a table near the back. This was the pub of choice for those who worked at Caledonia Interpol; it made them feel comfortable. A subterranean treehouse, by the name of Waxy O'Connor's. There were bars hidden throughout the underground pub, and it was easy to get lost there among the stained glass windows and dark wooden booths. The labyrinthine rooms and passageways often reminded them of the land of Faerie; their true home, and their eventual destination, once the human world ceased to be. For now, they walked the earth with humans, but Waxy's was a breath of home.

Dorian was a mystery to Leah. Even in the darkness of the pub, she noticed the sadness behind his eyes, a deep ocean chasm. His composure was as supernatural as he was. His refined attitude, dress sense, and gentlemanly demeanour made him undeniably attractive. Yet, he moved through the world as though he never noticed other people at all.

"I hope you don't mind my asking," she said, "It seems you could have anyone you wanted, but you're alone. Why?"

Dorian looked up from his drink and flashed a rare smile.

"We mate with humans," he said. "Selkies are male, and bisexual. We have two separate purposes, and only two. The first is to find someone who has been disappointed in love, and *comfort* them."

Leah grinned at the implication.

"The second," he continued, "is to fall in love with a human. Someone whose heart has been broken can cry seven tears into the sea and call a selkie lover. If this happens, we fall in love, forever."

"Sounds romantic," said Leah.

"Does it?" he said. "I suppose it must seem that way, to you. However, there is no *getting over it* for a seal-man. Once he has fallen, it is for the rest of his life. He cannot love another."

"I think I can empathise," Leah said. "So... who was your human?"

"A divorcée, in my case," said Dorian. "She cried seven tears into the sea. She didn't even realise she was doing it. I went to her and comforted her. I loved her, as only a selkie can. As you may know, this does not guarantee the love will be returned."

"Yes," Leah said dryly. "I know."

"Once her heart had mended, she left me," he said. He looked at Leah.

"What about you?" he asked. "I recognise heartbreak when I hear it."

Leah stared into her pint for a while. She had expected to run away from her past, everything still being so painful. And yet, with this selkie, the story poured out of her, as if her soul would be cleansed in the telling. Maybe this was selkie magic, too.

"He was... the love of my life," she managed. "I had never met anyone like him before. I was impressed with him. He was so stylish, you know, so at ease with himself and the world. Musical, a great dancer, everything I could ever want in a man.

He spent a lot of time away. With work, he said. Then, one day, he just didn't come home. And I found out that he hadn't been away at work."

Dorian nodded, as though he already knew the story.

"Oldest story in the book, really," she said, to show she knew it too. "But it's harder when it's your own."

"Yes," said Dorian. "The pain never really ends, through the centuries."

There was a pause. Leah stared at him.

"How old are you?" she asked.

"The seal-folk don't mark age," he replied, "but for your purposes, I was at the court of Louis XIV."

Leah stared at him.

"And what a pompous arsehole he was," Dorian added.

Leah laughed. He raised an eyebrow.

"Magnificent, though," he said. Leah shook her head.

"Isn't it difficult, working with a human?" she asked.

"On the contrary, we need humans," he replied. "Especially humans like yourself, who understand us."

"I don t think I ll ever understand you," she laughed, and drank her beer.

"More than most," Dorian said, following suit. His phone buzzed. Leah watched with amusement as the Victorian gentleman pulled a mobile phone out of a pocket in his tailcoat. He looked down at it.

"Time to go," he said.

"What?" she asked, suddenly alert. "Is there another body?"

"No," he said, showing her the phone. "The kelpie in the Clyde is being a nuisance, and we have to get it out."

Leah grabbed her coat and followed Dorian into the rainy night.

***

The night was cloudy and dark beside the river. Leah peered over the side of the wall into the water. She could barely see the ripples on the surface.

"Can you see anything?" she asked.

"Not yet," Dorian said.

Red eyes appeared beneath the water and were gone in an instant.

"Did you - " Leah began.

"-see that?" Dorian finished.

"Yes," they both said.

Suddenly, there was a loud roar, and a cascade of water. The monster reared out of the waves, soaking them in a deluge. It roared again, exposing rows of shark-like teeth. It looked like a great black dragon with a serpentine neck. The dull lights of the city glittered off of its black scales. Dorian took a step back. Leah planted her feet on the pavement, determined to stay just where she was.

"What now?" she hissed. And the monster began to sway, side to side. It wheezed, and snuffled loudly, water fountaining from its snout. Dorian stared hard at the creature, and then began to laugh. Leah turned to him in astonishment. The kelpie made some hooting noises that sounded almost musical. It swayed back and forth, ululating and whuffling.

"It's drunk, Miss Bishop," said Dorian. "It's singing along to the bagpipes."

"It's... what?" Leah said, looking at the monster, which made a *whrrrrrr* sound.

"It's drunk," Dorian repeated, grinning, "and it's purring. I think it needs to sober up, and get out of the river for now."

"Dorian," she said quietly. "This is a *kelpie*, the child-eating monster? Is this... is it safe? Shouldn't we take it out of here for good?"

Dorian looked at her and his smile faded.

"You're right, of course," he said. "It's dangerous, but it has lived in the Clyde since I can remember."

He sighed, and squared his shoulders.

"Nothing for it, then, is there?" he said.

And he removed his brocade tailcoat, his waistcoat, and his shirt. Leah turned away out of modesty, wondered why she had, and then resolutely turned around again because she pretty much lived for these sorts of opportunities. As a purely aesthetic exercise, of course.

Dorian was in the river. She hadn't seen him move or jump and she hadn't heard a splash. Still in the shape of a man, he cut through the water as though he were a part of it. He was beside the kelpie in a moment, laying a hand on its hide. It roared, startled, and looked down at the man beneath it, baring its great teeth.

"I wouldn't," Leah heard Dorian say, and then saw a flash of brilliant blue from his eyes. Leah thought she would never get used to that, so often she seemed to forget what he truly was. Dorian guided its head down towards the water, and whispered *drink*.

The kelpie froze, and became as docile as a lamb, drinking the water as directed. When it had finished, Dorian swam alongside it, guiding it to the stairs along the wall. It placed a claw upon the concrete as the selkie hauled himself up onto the stairs.

Leah wasn't sure how it happened. All she saw was the huge dragon-like head move downwards at Dorian, and she was suddenly right there, her fist connecting with its snout. The kelpie yelped in surprise and pain. It swung its massive head to look down at her. She stared at it, then crossed her arms. Water sluiced down onto her from the great creature's body, and she was completely drenched. Suddenly, she burst out laughing, and laughed loud, a sound of freedom and wonder.

Dorian smiled.

He then pulled the creature up the steps along with him. As it stepped onto dry land, its body folded in upon itself. A white horse stood in its place, the most beautiful Leah had ever seen. It swayed a little, and Dorian looked into its eyes.

"Walk it off," he said softly. "Do not bother the people of this city, or you will have to answer to us. We protect Glasgow. Remember me, and remember her. Be on your best behaviour, or we shall hear of it. *You do not want that.*"

❀ CHAPTER THREE ❀

His eyes flashed that brilliant blue again as he stood there, his hand on the horse's flank. The kelpie looked at Dorian for a long time, and then nickered, nuzzling his side. Dorian slapped the kelpie's flank, and the horse went on its way alone, swaying from side to side as it vanished into the distance.

Beautiful and deadly, thought Leah, *both of them.*

Then Dorian beamed at her, breaking the spell, and she smiled back. They both began laughing, and he swept a hand through his wet hair, shaking the water out of it. They walked back to Caledonia, talking about many things.

Chapter Four

The neon haze seemed to filter in and out. Dylan stared at the sign. He knew he could read. He could remember reading at some point. Time for the chippy, he thought. Too many £1.99 glasses of wine. He was a self-respecting ned, but he wouldn't say no to a bargain, wine or otherwise. Cheap alcohol was good alcohol, and he didn't care what anyone thought about his choice of beverage. It didn't make him any less of a man, or a ned; it made him resourceful and adaptive. Or so he told himself, anyway. Secretly, he just really liked wine, and even the swill they sold at this pub reminded him of his private love for the finer things.

He felt the soft pockets of his hoodie and was overjoyed to discover there was a packet of Mayfair cigarettes in them. He opened it and felt the deep disappointment of a drunk who doesn't have any more money to spend and has forgotten that he breathed his last smoke a while ago.

He stared up at the statue of a Highlander, standing in front of him and wearing a puzzled expression. Dylan furrowed his brow, trying to coax forth a memory of this statue. It didn't work. He couldn't remember when they had put this statue up, nor why it would have such a strange look on its face. In fact, he was certain he had never seen it before. Especially not right in front of his favourite Wetherspoon's. It was his favourite because they had the cheapest bottles of wine in Glasgow.

He wasn't even sure he'd been kicked out of the pub, he just knew that he'd collapsed in the doorway. Or in a doorway. Come to think of it, he wasn't sure where he was. Then the statue spoke to him.

"Pardon me," said the statue in the thickest *teuchter* accent Dylan had ever heard. Dylan gaped.

"Aye?" asked Dylan.

"Do you know the way to the cattle market?" the statue asked, in such heavily accented English and in such a carefully pronounced way that Dylan wondered if other countries had *teuchters*, too. In a flash of drunken brilliance, he realised *of course they must* and suddenly felt warm and connected to the rest of the world.

"Mate. Mate. Mate. Mate," Dylan said, then realised the record was skipping, adjusted and reset.

"Got a fag, mate?"

The statue didn't seem to understand him. Dylan sighed theatrically.

"D'you have a cigarette, pal?" he grumbled, enunciating every syllable.

"No," said the statue, then, pronouncing its words very carefully again, "*Do you know the way to the cattle market*?"

"Wit?" Dylan began to sober up.

"Cattle market?" Dylan repeated. "There's no' been a cattle market in Glasgow since Bonnie Prince Charlie died, God rest his soul."

Dylan felt that a bit of 3 a.m. patriotism was never amiss. The statue looked startled.

"Charles is dead?!" it shouted.

Dylan peered up at the statue. He now realized that standing in front of him was an honest-to-God Highland swordsman, like the kind he'd once seen on a television programme about the American Highland Games. He stared at the statue again. Flowing hair, strong muscles, a friendly and smiling face that nevertheless said *if you make a sudden move I will break you in half.*

"I'm Tearlach, of Glengoyne," said the Highlander, holding out his hand. "I follow Iain."

Dylan goggled at him. Of course that would be his name. He wondered vaguely who Iain was.

"Dylan," he said, and shook the other man's hand.

Tearlach took this opportunity to help him up.

"A bit too much drink, Dylan?" he grinned.

Dylan was horrified to note that the man looked like the cover of a romance novel. He was even wearing a kilt. Piercing blue eyes, perfect silhouette, the works. Dylan could only make a low sound in his throat.

"Nothing a good walk won't cure, let's go," Tearlach continued. "You Lowlanders never could hold your liquor."

In a daze, Dylan let Tearlach lead him down Sauchiehall Street.

Someone was going to have to explain everything to him again when he was sober.

Leaning on Tearlach's shoulder as the sun came up, Dylan led the man through the chain-link gate to his dreary block of council flats. He fished in his pocket for the key, and after a few heroic efforts, snagged it between two fingers. He pushed the door open, past piles of the Sun and the Daily Mail on the floor, and let Tearlach step past him. The Highlander stood in the kitchen in awe.

Dylan turned the tap on the sink and Tearlach stared in wonder as the water poured out. Dylan watched his new houseguest as the man hesitantly splashed water on himself from the sink. He seemed to suspect witchcraft. Dylan felt a little threatened in his masculinity by the fantasy Highland warrior in front of him.

"Sae d'you follow Rangers?" asked Dylan.

Tearlach looked up from the sink and stared at him.

"What does that mean?" he asked.

Dylan's mouth was working at finding words just as someone knocked on the door. He kept looking over his shoulder at Tearlach as he went to open it, only to gurgle in surprise at the beautiful young man with long curls standing on his doorstep.

"How many of you are there?!" cried Dylan, turning to look at Tearlach again. Tearlach shrugged.

"Dylan Stuart?" asked the young man. Dylan nodded, this

being a bit too much to take with a hangover.

"I'm Detective Inspector Magnus Grey. We'd like to have a talk with you down at the station," he said. "We'll need your Highlander to come along as well."

This being the last straw, Dylan held out his arms wordlessly, wrists together, and surrendered.

***

Leah walked into the station, and nearly straight into Magnus, who wore an indescribable expression.

"I think we have a situation," he said, and turned to reveal Dylan and Tearlach, the latter of whom was looking around the enormous library in wonder.

Leah was having a difficult time containing herself after the situation had been explained to her.

"I'm surprised there aren't hairy Scottish Highlanders wandering through every point in history, given their habit of time-travel," she laughed.

Tearlach looked at her, affronted.

"I'll have you know, madam, that I do shave. I am not a savage!" he said.

"Better than most men these days," she grinned.

Dylan rubbed his own hairless chin and glared around the room. Dorian put his hand to his head as if he had a headache.

"Can we focus, please?" he said. "This may be serious."

"Or it may not," Leah said. "You expect me to take this seriously? Here - we had better keep him away from feisty women, you know how time-travelling Highlanders love those."

Magnus flashed her one of his killer smiles.

"You'd better steer well clear, then, Leah," he said, and she winked at him.

"So let me get this straight," she said. "A time-travelling Highlander from the 18th century comes to Glasgow and the first person he meets is... a ned? I can't wait for the sex scene. I'm bringing popcorn."

At this, Dylan raised his head and seemed to pay attention for the first time.

"Oi!" he said. "What's wi' aw the prejudice? What kind o' polis station is this, anyway?"

He stared suspiciously around at the Jacobean library, which was unlike any police station he had ever seen.

"Stop. Please," said Dorian.

"Yeah, you'd better be quiet, or Dorian here will kill you with his laser beam eyes," said Leah, laughing.

"I saw someone die tonight," said Tearlach suddenly. The room went quiet.

Everyone looked at him. Dorian straightened, once again interested in the conversation.

"Where?" he asked.

"Just before I met Dylan," said Tearlach. "I went to help, but it was too late."

"Why didn't you say anything before?" asked Magnus.

"I didn't know what clan you were from," Tearlach replied. "Now that I know you are selkies, I don't mind telling, gentle creatures."

Leah nodded, amused. She knew that in the past, the Faeries were called The Good People, or gentle, or any other compliment, simply because they were terrifying and had immense power. It was one way that humans had tried to appease them and to protect themselves from the wrath of the Fae.

"How did you know they were selkies?" she asked. Tearlach shot her a confused look.

"Can't you see how they shimmer?" he asked.

Leah and Dylan stared at the selkies, and both shook their heads. Tearlach was horrified.

"Goodness, what are people teaching schoolchildren these days?" he said. "In my time it was wisdom taught by our elders."

"Not anymore, I'm afraid," Leah said. "We're taught they aren't real."

Tearlach gasped, and looked from Dorian to Magnus.

"Madam, do you have a death wish?!" he whispered to Leah.

"To say such things in the hearing of the Good People! They may look beautiful, but the seal-folk are fierce, and not to be trifled with!"

Leah looked at Dorian's slight, Victorian figure, and raised an eyebrow.

"I think we're getting sidetracked," Dorian said smoothly. "Tearlach, can you remember what you saw?"

Tearlach bowed to him.

"My deepest and most sincere apologies, gentle one, and for the human woman she cannot help her ignorance and lack of education," said Tearlach.

Leah's mouth dropped open, and she almost spoke, but thought better of it.

"I cannot say what happened, because I was too late to see it," Tearlach continued. "I held her as she expired. I think she found it a comfort, for she was having visions near the end."

"Visions?" asked Magnus. "What do you mean?"

"I think she thought me her lover, or husband," Tearlach said. "I did what I could, but it was too late."

"And why did you feel that you should share this with us?" asked Dorian. "Because we are Fair Folk?"

Tearlach looked from Dorian to Magnus.

"Because, my lord... she was one of you," he said.

"Did you recognise her species, Tearlach?" asked Magnus.

"Aye," he replied. "She was a brownie."

Dorian and Magnus exchanged a horrified look. Leah was puzzled, as brownies - the househelpers, cleaning each night in exchange for a bowl of milk, were probably the most benevolent of all the Fair Folk. Dorian and Magnus did not seem to notice her consternation: they were communicating on another plane of existence. Finally, one of them spoke.

"This means they are not just killing faeries," said Dorian. "They are killing innocents. They are killing the Attendants."

Chapter Five

nother day dawned in Glasgow, grey as the one before it, and colder. The news on the television was grim, as always, and Leah wondered why the faerie population insisted on mimicking the violence of the human one.

It seemed as though she could not study folklore without seeing it. The children's films and stories most people associated with folklore were far removed from the reality. Most adults with an interest in storytelling knew that folklore and faerie tales were almost entirely stories about monsters. If a song, or a poem, or a cautionary tale was not about a monster, it was certain to be about someone's death, or suffering. Faerie tales were usually used to warn people, or to teach a lesson. Even modern urban legends followed the familiar pattern of monster stories, serving as instruction manuals to live life safely and well. Another aspect of human nature seemed to be a love of the macabre. The most famous stories were often the bloodiest. In the same way that people loved the false fear of a roller coaster ride, so they had enjoyed horror stories since the days when those stories were spoken in hushed whispers around a campfire in the dark.

Leah lay with her fingers intertwined, head resting on her pillow, and considered the implications of all this. She picked up her phone and saw the time. It was getting late. She stretched, put her bare feet onto cool tiles and padded over to the kettle to make tea.

How I ended up here, I'll never know, she thought to herself, as she put the cup to her lips, *Here I am, a police officer in a bad dream of a city, all grit and broken glass. Why anyone would choose to live in this place I can't imagine - it's guaranteed suicide.*

She looked outside, at the rain and mist that greeted her. The city was a dark place, but she had often noted that the grass and trees were a brilliant, jewelled green.

And somehow, I'm still here, she thought.

Without him, but I'm still here.

***

Leah went into the kitchen at the station and saw that Dorian and Magnus were arguing. She leaned against the wall and drank her tea, smiling to herself. The station's kitchen was well-stocked and she found herself almost mainlining tea. Dorian was no different. He devoted many hours to delicately sipping at cups of Earl Grey. His dedication to, and consumption of, this type of tea was elevated to an art form.

She had asked him, once, why this was.

"Because it's mine," he had stated.

This was very puzzling, and as she watched him now, with his cup of Earl Grey, arguing with his brother, she nearly dropped her own tea in realisation.

Because it's mine.

Earl Grey.

Dorian...

This revelation sent her mind reeling, just as Magnus's voice raised and broke through her thoughts.

"Look, just because you've already been Taken there's no need for all this- " Magnus was saying.

"It has nothing to do with that," said Dorian impatiently. "I'm just saying that you ought to be more circumspect, especial-ly around here. These aren't human women, Magnus, *they are monsters,* and if they find out that you've been unfaithful, they are going to kill you."

Magnus rolled his eyes.

"All right, all right," said Magnus. "But it *is* because you're Taken. Only the Taken dress like Victorian dandies."

Dorian gave him a once-over, putting more contempt into

his expression than every cat on earth.

"Better than whatever excuse for clothing *you* happen to be wearing," he sniffed.

"No complaints yet," grinned Magnus, straightening Dorian's coat and stalking off.

"Trouble in paradise?" Leah asked, as she walked over. Dorian sneered.

"*Brothers*," he said. "He's coming to help us today. Much as I hate to admit it, he does have a way with the... type of *person* we need to interview."

"When you say person you mean-"

"Humans, yes," said Dorian. "A supernatural would rather speak to me anytime. However, Magnus can speak to humans more readily than I can. I suppose most humans don't like speaking with a man in a Victorian waistcoat, especially one as thin and pretty as I am."

You got that right, thought Leah. Dorian stared at her. Too late, she remembered he could hear her thoughts. He raised an eyebrow, and went on.

"The desire to beat me up is far too strong. Besides, I find them... distasteful."

"Well, what about me?" Leah asked. "I'm a detective, and I'm human."

Dorian smiled a strange smile.

"You're *different*," he said, as if that explained everything.

Leah wondered how she was meant to feel about that.

***

Sometimes a night in Glasgow ends well past the morning.

Down by the Clyde, gulls swooped and shrieked, as the ferryboats started their morning runs. It was peaceful, and quiet; the wind lifted the newspapers and rubbish along the riverside. The air of the city sometimes nearly matched the architecture, a kind of dull reddish-beige. Everything was washed out. There was also a smell, one that was uniquely Glasgow; the sour flavour in the air from the breweries that rode the winds of the city.

Revellers from the night before stood around talking or lazing on the steps down by the water. Glasgow was not a romantic city. It was functional, and had needed to be for a good many years. However, if a romantic spot was needed at short notice, the edge of the Clyde at sunrise was probably as close as you were likely to get. A young couple was embracing by the river, lost in each other. Magnus walked straight up to them.

"Excuse me," he said. "We'd like to talk to you about an investigation."

The man glared at him, as the woman turned around. He was clearly unhappy to be disturbed. *She* saw Magnus, and her entire demeanour changed; any anger completely evaporated. She was suddenly all too willing to speak, although her boyfriend continued to favour them with a threatening look. Dorian and Leah hung back and stood near the river, letting Magnus do all the talking.

"Did you see anything strange last night?" he asked.

The woman stared at him, and then looked him up and down. She stepped closer to him, almost intimate.

"No, but I wish I'd seen you," she said. "You're *gorgeous*."

Magnus smiled into her expression like a predator. Her lips parted, and her eyes went wide.

Leah sighed in annoyance. Dorian questioned her with a look. She shook her head.

"It's just..." she said. "It makes me feel so... *unoriginal* for finding him attractive."

Dorian half-smiled at her, which was for him tantamount to throwing his head back and laughing.

Magnus grinned at the woman as she smiled back coyly. Her boyfriend looked concerned for the first time.

"Come on," he said urgently. "Let's get out of here."

She pushed her boyfriend away roughly, still smiling at Magnus with a hungry look in her eyes. Leah started to feel concerned. This woman looked as if she wanted to tear into the young seal-man. Magnus had turned back to speak to Dorian when the girl laid a hand on his arm.

"I did see something," she said, eager to keep Magnus interested. "Some girl left the club with this lad, and they never came back."

"Can you describe them to me?" asked Magnus. This time, she put her arm in his.

"Maybe somewhere more private?" she breathed.

Her boyfriend stepped between them, alarmed, and pushed them apart.

"No, definitely not," he said, holding them both at arm's length.

"Sir, this is official police business," said Leah. "Don't interfere."

"I don't care!" he replied.

"Sir..." said Dorian, and he placed his hand on his brother's shoulder, anchoring himself against Magnus. "I believe the lady said this was *official police business*."

A wind breathed along the Clyde, first like feathers, then like fury.

Leah backed away as she saw the selkies... *change*.

Their eyes turned a bright ice blue. As the wind began to blow a gale, whipping Magnus's long hair around his beautiful face, the Clyde foamed as though preparing for a hurricane. Dorian and Magnus had almost always looked human, but now, Leah could not understand how she had ever seen them as men. She had never seen such an expression on the face of a human being.

The people of the seal.

Ancient, furious anger.

Stiletto images stabbed with the force of pure memory.

The green and cold sea.

The loneliness of a shingle beach on some unknown Scottish island.

The anger of the clans, and the pain of their broken hearts.

The images all came down in a wild and rapid heartbeat, swift and sure.

Leah knew that the angry young man felt every emotion and the depths of the sea in his veins.

The last feeling, as the wind died completely to a stillness Glasgow did not often know, was of calm, of being cared for by the lonely sentinels, the seal-men who stood guard and healed the heartbreak of the Scottish people.

"Wow," said the girl, who had evidently experienced the onslaught of all these emotions, if inadvertently. "So, are you single?"

The seal-men, whose eyes had died down to their natural everyday brown colour, turned as one body to the woman, and said *No* and *Yes* at the same time.

***

The city was full of old man's pubs. They had the cheapest prices on alcohol and the best banter in town, but they tended to be frequented by pensioners who preferred the pubs of their youth to the loud and glitzy alternatives elsewhere in Glasgow. Some of these places were truly ancient, and indicative of the solid history of Scotland. The Castle Vault, Tennant's, and countless others could be found on heritage lists. If Glasgow liked anything, it liked a good old man's pub.

Aonghas was sitting at the sticky bar of the Piper's Rest, which was a very special kind of old man's pub. Some of the old men here were positively ancient... not that you could tell from their faces. Aonghas was young, or at least he looked that way. Old man's pubs didn't actually discriminate on the basis of age. The booze was cheap, people kept to themselves until it was time for a cigarette, and by the late evening so many fights would have broken out and so many new friendships made (forgotten by the following morning) that they didn't care what age you were, so long as your money was multi-coloured and occasionally stained red.

This was a pub for supernaturals. Although it had both human and fae patrons, the humans just thought it was a run-down place, a nondescript pub like all the others, a hole in the wall in some random part of the city. The bar itself was in the centre of the room, a large black wooden behemoth from older days, with a huge bell hanging above it. In other pubs, this bell was for ringing at closing time. At the Piper's Rest, you had better pray to whatever gods you had that it never rang at all.

Patrons sat in the booths along the walls. Everything about the Piper's Rest looked like the usual Scottish heritage pub, aside from the fact that they poured more than beer, wine, and whisky behind the counter. And there was something strange about the barman.

There were also two doors. Sometimes humans stumbled into the wrong one, looking for the bathroom, and didn't reappear for decades, if they did at all.

Aonghas, like Dylan, was what the people of Glasgow tended to refer to as a *ned*. They were the Glasgow poor, inhabiting council estates and other areas, almost in a defiant way, holding tight to their fame and status as the dangerous types of the city. They were frequently the despair of Glasgow, but had existed since the city began, as Aonghas knew all too well.

Glaschu. Glasgow. The Dear Green Place.

It made Aonghas smile as he drank his pint, though he already had a few bottles of Buckfast in his satchel. Funny old world, he thought. It had been years since he'd taken the satchel on any kind of quest, but it always stored provisions he'd never actually purchased or picked up anywhere. He didn't remember when it had stopped offering succulent meats, jugs of wine, rare cheeses and the spices of faraway lands, but he missed them. These days, it was Buckfast bottles, Irn-Bru, and (sometimes) a fish and chip dinner or a curry.

His shining, dragonfly-veined wings slowly unfolded. They were beautiful, heartbreaking, and completely incongruous. As he shook the rain from them, no one in the pub even gave him a second look.

Aonghas was a Trooping Faerie. These were the Fae that

marched together, beautiful and brilliant; the faeries of folk-lore that snatched children from their cribs, tempted young men and women, and were the reason many ancient homes in Scotland and Ireland were built with their front and back doors facing each other, to offer the Trooping Faeries free passage. Aonghas once had glorious long shining brown hair and had been clothed in green raiment, seducing young maidens in secluded bowers. Those women would then bear his half-Fae children, more beautiful than any human could have imagined. The children often did not realise they were magical, and only a strange sixth sense and vague dreams of ancient songs would indicate their parentage.

These days, things had changed. Aonghas was beautiful still, but he no longer resembled his former self. His head was shaved and he wore Celtic colours. That was not his choice, but his green robes had faded, folded, and become a green tracksuit with a matching green-and-white-striped scarf. A shamrock tattoo had appeared on his neck at some point but he had no idea how it got there. There were no forests anymore. Everything had turned to broken concrete. Now, he was reduced to Sauchiehall on a Saturday night and going out on the pull, often settling for the lowest common denominator at the club.

Aonghas no longer cared. He had given up.

As Scotland had changed, so too had the Trooping Faeries. He thought of the powerful and terrifying Fair Folk, child-stealers and rulers of time, now working as temps or finding themselves, like him, bored and unhappy with modern life. He even knew one who had become a successful drag queen - it paid well, and the Trooping Faeries *were* preternaturally beautiful.

As he lifted his glass to take another drink, musing on the unfairness of it all, he found something stuck to the bottom of his glass. He made a sound of disgust - ned or not, the Trooping Faeries disliked a mess, even in pubs. He then saw that it was a piece of paper with *Aonghas* written on it in his ancient language. He stared at his own name, glowing through the yellow of the beer with the light golden sheen of early autumn forests.

🌸 CHAPTER FIVE 🌸

Slowly, he peeled the paper from the bottom of his glass and unfolded it. There was one word written upon the paper:

Dublin

The bartender came around to see if his Trooping Faerie customer wanted anything else. He found nothing but a half-drunk pint and the Fae gold that Aonghas had, once again, tried to use as currency. He grunted and lifted the sheaf of leaves, putting them on a paper spike along with all the others he had left. The bartender had been around awhile, and he lived in hope that one day, Aonghas would finally settle his tab.

***

Later that day, Leah walked with Dorian.

"What happened earlier..." Leah began, and trailed off.

Her friend - was he her friend now, as well as her partner? She supposed he must be. They did have some things in common, even if he did wear white gloves all day long. Dorian smiled.

"Yes, I thought you might ask about that," he said. "It's one kind of magic that the seal-people can do. Our spell, so to speak - the selkie cantrip. I trust that you were not as affected by it as that young couple was."

"It was intense for me," said Leah.

"The cantrip causes different reactions in different people," he said. "What it primarily does is remind people they have an underused conscience, and then, they pay for it. All the guilt they should feel, they feel all at once, and they remember the long history of who our people were, and they are ashamed. Is this what you felt?"

"No," Leah admitted. "I saw the ocean, and a beach, and the sadness of the people, and the loss."

Dorian nodded.

"That is indicative of a good character," he said. "But the cantrip is, in its own way, very effective nevertheless. For someone from Scotland, it reminds them of their history."

"What about criminals? Like the serial killer we are dealing with? Wouldn't it work on them?" Leah asked.

"Well, someone must first have a conscience for it to work properly," he said. "It doesn't always work on supernaturals. But this killer - I doubt even the cantrip would make him feel what he has done."

"You are certain about the killer being a sociopath, then? No motive other than madness?" Leah asked.

"Well, it is always possible that the killer is just trying to make it look that way," said Dorian. "In a tight corner, the cantrip controls the weather. Particularly at sea. Some of my people have been known to sink ships in storms because of their anger at the heartless slaughter of the seals."

"Selkies can control the weather?" Leah asked. "Can you make the sun come out?"

In response, Dorian fixed his gaze on the sky. Warmth spread across the city and people blinked in the sudden light. Leah looked at Dorian and grinned. Dorian's eyes were half-closed, almost as if he had gone to sleep, and in the sunlight he looked blissed out... like a seal basking, she realised.

"Why don't the seal-people do this every day? Make Scotland a tropical paradise?" Leah asked, amazed.

Dorian looked at her as if she were crazy. The clouds moved in and covered the sun.

"And destroy our perfect skin?" he asked. "Besides, no one in Britain ever wants to be warm. The sun is a myth, Leah. Never forget that."

To her surprise, he winked.

"Did you just wink at me?" she asked.

"I might have," he said, and she laughed.

***

Dorian held the door open for Leah when they returned.

They exchanged a look when they saw that Chief Ben was waiting by Leah's desk with a file folder.

"Good morning, sir," Dorian bowed. "What can we do for you?"

Chief Ben handed him the file.

"Milo asks that you pay him a visit," he said. "He says there's something downstairs you need to see."

"Very well," said Dorian.

"Downstairs?" asked Leah, who had only ever seen the main room. "Who's Milo?"

"He's our forensic pathologist," said Dorian. "One of them, anyway."

"You have a forensic pathologist for *faeries*?" asked Leah.

"Of course," said Dorian, puzzled. "How else would we extract DNA?"

Her eyes were round.

"Well," she said, "it looks like I've been remiss in my studies."

***

Dorian led her down a series of passageways into the basement. It felt like the kind of place that generally starred in films about haunted asylums. The hallways were wide and empty, echoing their footfalls. Mysterious doors and openings of various sizes and shapes led off the main artery.

"This is the Labyrinth," Dorian explained. "It can be very dangerous. Its boundaries are unknown. Be very careful of the turns you take here."

"Okay," said Leah.

"And watch out for the Minotaur," Dorian added. Leah stopped short.

"There's a Minotaur in the Labyrinth?" she asked.

"Yes," said Dorian. "*The* Minotaur. Transfer from Greece, a very long time ago. There are things, and beings, in Milo's lab that a lot of people would like to get their hands on."

She followed him, down several corridors and through

countless doorways. Each door was different. Some were small, too small for anyone human to enter. Some were ornate, and some were plain. A few were so tall she could not see the top of the doorframe. She looked around in wonder, curious as to where they might lead.

Something like fog began to settle around them.

"Keep close to me," said Dorian.

Leah tried, but the fog was getting thicker and soon she could see nothing at all.

"Dorian?" she called out hesitantly.

She turned, and saw a door off to her right. She walked over to it and turned the handle. She stepped inside a room, and the first thing she saw was the silhouette of a bull's head, as her eyes began to adjust to the darkness.

The Minotaur.

Leah tried to duck back out of the doorway, hiding from the huge form of the Minotaur just as it turned around. Her back to the wall, she stared at the monster. There was music playing in the background...

Leah abruptly recognised the original version of *Walk This Way*. And then noticed where she was. It was a barn, filled with classic cars in various states of repair. A mechanic's shop. The Minotaur was working on a '67 Mustang fastback.

"Hey," it said, in a Midwestern American accent. "Grab a beer if you want, there's cold ones in the fridge."

Leah's heart slowed to a steadier pace. She edged towards the refrigerator and cautiously took out a beer. She turned around and leaned against the wall, watching the man work. The Minotaur was built, with a wide chest and muscular arms. He was wearing blue jeans and a black t-shirt, with a pack of cigarettes rolled up in one sleeve. Everything about him and the barn seemed perfectly normal - well, American-normal - aside from the fact that he had a bull's head.

"Well, don't just stand there," said the Minotaur. "What's your name?"

"Leah. Leah Bishop."

"Hey Leah."

"Are you... are you American?" she asked. "I thought the Minotaur was from Crete."

"Oh yeah," said the Minotaur, "Crete was a long time back. Wow. I haven't thought about Crete in years."

He took a long drink of his beer, and disappeared under the hood of the Mustang again.

"But yeah, this is America," he said. "Been here for ages. Like the land, the cars, the open road."

Leah drank her beer.

"I don't know about you," she said. "But I'm in the Labyrinth at Caledonia Interpol, in Scotland. You're the guard for Milo's lab."

The Minotaur stood up and wiped the black engine grease from its arms.

"They haven't told you much about how all of this works, have they?" he said. "Yeah, I guard that lab. And lots of other places. Your Interpol isn't just one place, it's *everywhere*."

"So all the doors in the Labyrinth -" she began.

"Actually lead somewhere, yeah," he said. "Some places are on earth, some places are way further than that."

He crossed his arms and looked at her, thumbing at the label on his beer bottle. She found herself wanting to know what his human face would have looked like. *Probably hot*, she assumed.

"You took a wrong turn," he said. "This time, you got me. Next time, you're not gonna be so lucky."

He led her to another door.

"Here you go," he said. "Hope to see you again sometime. Stop by when you can."

"Thanks," said Leah, and walked through the door.

She found herself outside the door to Milo's lab. When she turned to look behind her, the door had vanished.

"Leah!" Dorian said, relieved. "I thought I lost you!"

"Sorry," she said. "I met the Minotaur. He's kind of hot."

Dorian gave her a strange look.

"In the future," he said, "if we get separated again, or you need to come to the lab on your own, these are the directions."

He set a piece of paper in her hand, a note written out in beautiful Victorian cursive.

Left, right. Eight steps forward. The gold key in the silver lock. The small door, set in the larger one. Don't open the small door. Through the large door, down past three turns, right, right, stop and turn widdershins. Place your bare palm on the wall.

"Thanks," she said.

"Let's go talk to Milo," he said. "Don't wander off."

"Yes, boss," she said, and grinned at him.

Dorian turned a corner and pushed a door open.

Leah saw that the forensics lab was not like most she had visited. The entire room was filled with mysterious equipment, vials and complicated glass enclosures of varying colour and size. The room was filled from end to end with beakers and bubbling liquid in tubes.

There were countless cages filled with tiny and strange creatures, and as she passed by, they shouted or squeaked at her, vying for attention. She peered into one of the cages, where a fluffy, triangular creature with enormous eyes stared out at her and made tiny *whoooot whoooot* sounds.

The lab was so fascinating that she noticed the men in lab coats last of all. Two figures were studiously working, unaware of their arrival, one bent over some paperwork, while the other examined something under a microscope. Leah was secretly overjoyed to see that the man at the microscope had a long yellow-orange fishtail. She had read about the *ceasg*, the only mer-people in Scottish folklore, but she knew they were unpredictable creatures. They would either grant three wishes, or eat souls, depending upon their mood.

"May I present Milo and Geoffrey," said Dorian with great ceremony. Neither of the men bothered to look up. Dorian grew impatient.

"What men are you, that you do not bow to a lady?" he demanded. The *ceasg* waved Dorian's words away.

"In a moment, Dorian," said the *ceasg*, named Milo. "I'm just looking for something... "

He glanced up, and saw Leah for the first time. She had a chance to examine him further. He wore thick glasses and had brown curling hair. The lithe, muscular human half of his body was highlighted in burnished gold; it traced the lines of his bones and dusted the hollow of his throat.

Despite all this, he looked like a total nerd.

"Oh my!" he said. "I am sorry, how rude." The merman managed a bow.

"Hello, and welcome," said the one named Geoffrey, looking over his glasses. He caught sight of Leah and his mouth dropped open. He was tall and gawky, in rumpled clothing, but there was something indescribably sweet about him, like a baby bird. He seemed instantly starstruck by her.

"Leah Bishop," she said, by way of introduction.

Geoffrey beamed at her.

"Dorian, we need to make sure that the crime scenes are accessible for me," Milo was saying. "If I can't get to them, there isn't much use, is there?"

"Indeed," Dorian agreed. "You are absolutely right, Milo. We are working on it."

Leah noticed a wheelchair in the corner. She realised that, unlike in films, mer-people were unable to change when they were out of the water. If people could magically grow working legs, that would be wonderful, but apparently magic did not always work that way.

"Yes, well," said Dorian. "What have you got for us, Milo?"

"Well, Geoffrey and I were having some lunch..." he began, and noticed that Geoffrey was off in his own world, staring at Leah. "*Geoffrey! Pay attention!*"

"Ahem, yes," said Geoffrey, shaking his head. "Apologies."

Milo looked at the photographs laid out across the table and sighed.

"*Geoffrey*, you've gotten *mustard* on the crime scene photos," he said, exasperated. He looked up at the selkie.

"I really don't know what I can do, Dorian," said Milo. "I know he has seniority but he's just so... *distracted*... all the time."

Geoffrey had returned to staring at Leah. This was beginning to get uncomfortable.

"If you're hungry," he said, "I think I have half a sandwich lying around -"

Leah smiled and shook her head.

"*Geoffrey,* " said Milo, in a warning tone, and then turned to Dorian. "See what I mean?"

"Indeed," sniffed Dorian.

"If you're not busy later..." Geoffrey began.

"*Geoffrey!*"

"Ah yes," Geoffrey said, collecting his thoughts. "The thing is... what we've found - it isn't human."

Dorian looked at them both curiously.

"Not entirely, that is," said Milo. "Modern genetics mean that it's relatively painless to compare the DNA from the killer to our database of supernatural DNA."

"So the killer is a supernatural?" asked Dorian.

"Well, it has all the genes you'd expect in a healthy human," said Geoffrey.

"However, it also has genes that we know to be of a supernatural origin - like a vampire, or a werewolf," finished Milo.

"Or - begging your pardon, Dorian - like you," said Geoffrey. "But that's where we run into problems."

"While the non-human genes are close to genes of supernatural origin," said Milo, "they aren't identical to any on file. We can't tell you what any of these genes do. I would love to be able to tell you, for example, what gene lets a selkie detect heartbreak, but supernatural genomics is nowhere near that stage."

"So... what does all this mean?" asked Leah.

"It means," said Milo, sighing, "I have no idea who, or what, is killing the Fae."

"So..." said Leah. "This is a new kind of monster?"

"Yes." said Milo, clearly glad to be on familiar ground again.

"Monsters all have to come from somewhere. We were all created, once upon a time. And not only is this creature new, I'd
estimate its abilities are more potent than anything we've ever
seen. You're basically fighting a smart bomb with a sword. The
selkies and other ancient races are nowhere near as *technologi-
cally advanced* as this one - if you can think of magic that way."

"If that is the case," said Dorian, "we will need to find a new
way to fight."

Chapter Six

The sun had deigned to emerge through the endless grey of the Glasgow skies. Leah walked out of Caledonia Interpol into the sunlight, where she stood blinking for a moment.

She was surprised when she saw Geoffrey sitting on one of the black benches that made up a circle outside of the back entrance to St. Enoch station, next to the shopping centre. Geoffrey looked up and saw her, then smiled and waved. She smiled back and walked over to him.

"Miss Bishop!" he said. "I am so glad to see you! I know you usually walk by here at lunchtime - and..."

"How did you know that?" asked Leah, her brows drawing together.

Geoffrey's face turned bright red.

"Well, you see, I, well," he stammered. "I just noticed, is all."

She sat down beside him.

She hadn't seen anyone this awkward in years and she found it rather endearing.

"I bought an extra sandwich, just for you," he said earnestly. "I hope you like coronation chicken, I... oh, dear. I seem to have sat on it."

He stared at the sad little flattened sandwich with such a morose expression that Leah laughed.

"Please, Miss Leah, I'm sorry," he said. "It's just... I get so nervous."

"It's all right," she said. "Let me get us some lunch. Stay here, I'll be right back."

Geoffrey looked as if he was about to argue. He clamped his mouth shut, wanting to preserve some semblance of dignity.

Leah returned with two tikka masalas and cans of Irn-Bru

from the chippy around the corner. She handed him a box and a can, and flipped open the lid of her own container. She stuck a fork in the rice, mixing it with the curry.

"There you are," she said. "I hope you like tikka masala. It looks like you could use a hot lunch."

He ate hungrily, and nodded.

"I don't get a lot of time at home," he said. "I'm always in the lab with Milo, and it's a 24/7 job."

"Where do you live?" asked Leah.

"Over by Cowcaddens," he said. "It's just a little bedsit. Empty. I... don't like going home alone."

He stared down into his curry, as if he had said too much, lifting his fork to his mouth automatically.

"I live alone too," she said. "In a hotel room. I don't like going there either."

They were both quiet for a while.

"Where are you from?" she asked.

"Basingstoke," he mumbled around his food. "I grew up there. Nothing much to tell, really. I did well in school, I went to university, I got the job at Caledonia Interpol, and that's all. If my life was a book, you'd only want to read it to put yourself to sleep."

"I'm sure that's not true," she said. "I get the feeling you have stories to tell."

Geoffrey finally looked up again.

"Would you... would you care to join me for dinner sometime?" he asked. "Maybe I could tell you some of them?"

Leah considered this. She hadn't gone out in ages, and it was nice to be asked. He wasn't exactly her type, but it would be nice to try with someone who was so clearly interested.

"That sounds great," she said. "I'd love to. What time?"

"Oh!" he said, startled, inadvertently knocking the remainder of his curry on the ground.

"Oh!" he repeated. "You said yes!"

He stared down at the curry as if it had betrayed him. Then he looked up at her, and she was laughing. A clear, joyful sound. He smiled, and laughed with her. Leah realised she had laughed more in the few days of work at Caledonia Interpol than she ever had in her years with Adam.

"Friday, seven o'clock?" Geoffrey asked, emboldened. Leah, still smiling, nodded.

"As long as we can keep you from knocking things over," she said.

"Well, I'm not making any promises." said Geoffrey, and grinned.

Leah laughed again. He stood up awkwardly and offered her his hand.

"I really must get back to work," he said. "But you enjoy your day, Miss Leah. Thank you for the curry."

Leah smiled.

"See you Friday." she said.

He blushed to the tips of his ears.

"Yes, see you Friday," he replied.

Leah watched him walk off, and shook her head, grinning.

***

The city was bustling in the sun, and people seemed happier than usual. Leah sat at a table at an outdoor cafe and had a glass of sparkling wine. She had never noticed how beautiful some of the older architecture was up close, or the way people smiled in the rarity of sunshine.

After she paid, her walk back to the hotel was more leisurely than it had been in the past. She noticed that the usual tang and chill of the Glasgow air was touched with the warmth of summer. The trees along the river had begun to bud, the green leaves pushing out. Soon the city would be filled with green, and litters of cherry blossom petals swirling on the breeze. She went up the stairs to her room, unlocked the door, and fell onto the bed. For the first night in a long time, the whisky bottle remained untouched on the table.

***

Leah awoke feeling refreshed and happy. She went and had a shower, got dressed, and met Dorian as he was coming into the hotel lobby.

"Good morning!" she sang, and he looked at her curiously.

"Have you had a good night, Miss Bishop?" he asked.

"Yes, I suppose I have," she said. "Call me Leah, Dorian. We're partners."

Dorian smiled briefly.

"Very well, then. Leah," he said. "Are you ready for work?"

"As I'll ever be."

The sun was bright, and the streets were crowded. It was the weekend and many people were out looking at the sights.

Leah sighed happily.

"Your heart is healing," said Dorian. It was not a question.

"I think it is," said Leah. "Geoffrey asked me on a date yesterday."

"Interesting," he said. "Is this the cause of your happiness?"

"Well," she paused, "not the date itself, no. It's just that for months I was feeling quite down and worthless. It feels good to have something to look forward to."

"Leah," said Dorian. "You were never worthless."

Leah grinned at her partner.

"Thank you, Mr. Grey," she said, and he laughed. "I do hope that you invite me to afternoon tea one day, sir."

"You are always welcome at my table," he said, with a bow. She looked at him in his trim tailcoat.

"What happens if we need to apprehend a suspect?" she asked. "Are you going to wear your gloves? Do we have any weapons?"

Dorian looked at her curiously.

"Didn't you read the manual?" he asked. Her eyebrows shot up.

"There's a manual?"

"It's sent out with all the hiring documents. Didn't you receive it?"

Leah thought back to the sad day back in Edinburgh when

the handsome man had come to her door.

"Now that you mention it," she said. "I did receive a packet. From a very handsome man, I might add."

"That would be one of the Trooping Faeries," he said, "or elves, if you like."

"Oh," she said, sad that she hadn't recognised a Faerie from the start. Now, she thought she'd know one anywhere.

***

Later that night, she dug through her things and found the ripped packet. She shook everything out onto the floor. And there it was. She must have been too depressed, drowning and looking for anything to haul herself out of the water, to have noticed anything but the job invitation.

CALEDONIA INTERPOL

Welcome
Please read with caution, as pages are liable to burst into flame

Startled by this piece of advice, Leah gingerly opened to the first page.

Welcome, distinguished creature, to your new life at Caledonia Interpol. Here, you will find an environment that celebrates diversity. We do not discriminate based on race, religion, creed, gender or multiple genders or non-genders thereof, sexuality, number of appendages, or species of monster. We strive to be the thin red line between humans and the dangers they still face from our kind. Our goal is for humans to believe the monster and ghost stories are memories, fictions from a long-ago past. If you are devoted to the cause, you will find a home here at Caledonia.

In these pages, you will find instructions about what will be required of you, and the things you will need to work with us.

You are kindly asked to refrain from the use of magic, and to learn to blend in with humans. Attempt to cultivate a love for tea, if you do not already have this. Humans are much more confident and reassured by tea drinking. Coffee is a secondary choice, but also useful, especially if you are eventually transferred to the Americas.

Some humans enjoy shouting incoherent things at you in the street. This is a normal pastime for many occupants of Glasgow; pay it no mind. It is entirely possible they can see your true form, but do not let this disturb you. Even if they tell others, most humans will not believe them anyway.

Leah laughed. She flipped through the pages, saw some chapter headings:

What is a Trouser Press? and *Queue Jumping: the New Horror.*

Then she discovered what she was looking for:

Weapons

She opened the page.
It was blank.
It was there, and it was blank. She turned the page. A new chapter entitled *Christmas Crackers and other Terrifying Cultural Phenomena.* She turned back. And in tiny letters at the top of the page, she saw:

fill in the blank

"Great," she said to herself. "Monsters are their own weapons. I suppose they never thought to provide for a human recruit."

***

She pushed the doors open at the station, and found Dorian contemplating the wall while drinking out of a tiny cup.

"What is this supposed to mean?" she asked, pointing at the page in the manual that said *fill in the blank*. Dorian set his cup down in a tiny saucer.

"Very good, that," he said, indicating the cup. "Pixies collect it from bees. Honeycomb tea."

Leah stared at him.

"Why don't you just go buy honey at the supermarket?" she asked.

"Why should I do that when I can have honeycomb tea harvested by pixies?" he replied, stoic as always.

Leah thought about this.

"Fair point," she said. "But don't change the subject - what does this mean?"

"Exactly what it says," said Dorian. "Generally, at Caledonia, we don't have weapons issued to us. We write down the weapons we have at our disposal, and then Chief Ben figures out a way to neutralise them if necessary."

Leah sat down in the chair across from him.

"Neutralise them?" she asked. "Why?"

"Some of us have powers that aren't exactly safe," he said. "You've seen what the selkies are capable of - and that was incredibly controlled, as Magnus and I worked together during the cantrip in order to keep our respective powers in check. It is a kind of ballet, to ensure the power does not get out of hand. Since the police force was created to help humanity, it is important that officers are unable to use any of their natural weaponry for evil - given that we formed a police force in order to prevent just such an occurrence."

"Well, what about me?" she asked. "I'm human! I'm weaponless."

Dorian lifted the tiny cup again and sipped from it.

"Are you?" he asked.

Chapter Seven

Piles of paperwork seemed just as common for the Fae police as it was for their human counterparts. Leah sat filling out forms until her eyes blurred. Suddenly, a steaming mug of milky tea appeared in front of her.

"Let's take a break," said Dorian.

She nodded, and took the mug with her into the kitchen. Two pixies were there, arguing.

"Thank you for the tea," Dorian said gently. "Miss Bishop and I need the room now."

The pixies bowed to him, and flew out the door, still arguing with each other. Leah was charmed and amused; everything here was still a surprise.

"I am going to tell you a story," said Dorian. "Perhaps it will help."

"Go on," said Leah, drinking her tea.

"Long ago," he began, "I met a man named Oscar Wilde."

Leah stared at him.

"What, *the* Oscar Wilde?" she asked.

"Yes," Dorian said. "I was familiar with his name, of course; it was hard for one not to hear of Oscar Wilde at that time. He was a celebrity. We spent an afternoon drinking in a café, discussing the world. I admit that I found the man fascinating. He had a brilliant mind, and as our conversation went on, I could not help but hint at what I was, if only to see what the great writer would make of it."

"Amazing," said Leah.

"I asked him - hypothetically, of course - what he thought a man would do if he were granted eternal youth and beauty. We discussed how such a man would behave, given the ability to have anything he wanted, and being stripped of all consequences - disease, old age, death, punishment. We went back and forth about whether such a man would sink into depravity and sin, or if he could find something greater to hold on to and overcome the temptations offered by such power. The day grew to a close and we parted ways. As he left, Wilde was speaking of committing everything we had discussed to a book on the nature of man - a novel."

Leah's eyes grew large.

"At the time, I wondered if anything would come of it," Dorian said. He smiled.

"So... you're telling me that *Oscar Wilde* wrote *The Picture of Dorian Gray* about you?!" she cried.

"Yes," said Dorian simply. He wore a strange expression, and Leah was startled to recognise that it was a look of muted pride.

"Or, at least," Dorian amended, "about our conversation. He certainly named the character after me."

Leah shook her head.

"But why the spelling?" she asked. "Yours is Grey with an E, isn't it?"

Dorian smiled again.

"Ah, yes," he said. "I'm sure Mr. Wilde did not know the spelling. We only met the once. It's a bit of a joke, our surname. All selkies use the surname Grey. No other species of seal can be a selkie."

"All right," she said. "But what does that have to do with weapons?"

"My power, Leah," he said, "can be misused, just like any other kind of power. The point of the discussion Oscar and I had, back then, was that despite power, wealth, and beauty, it is not a foregone conclusion that someone will behave with depravity. There are stronger things."

"You mean love?" asked Leah.

"I mean love, yes, but more than that," he said. "You must start by thinking of uncommon things as weapons. There is a great deal of strength in ephemeral things. Speaking as one of them, I should know. Brute force is not always what is required.

❀ CHAPTER SEVEN ❀

If you feel the need to discover what your weapons are, you must start thinking like the Fae, who without axes, swords, or guns, are nevertheless more powerful than any weapon humans have managed to create. Humans have power as well, but it is not in their weaponry, and that is where you need to start looking. What is it you have that we don't? Why are you, Leah Bishop, valuable to a police force of the most powerful creatures that have ever existed, if you are truly *just human* and weaponless?"

Leah sat quietly, and sipped her tea. She didn't know. She was happy that she had been chosen and that she was now aware of this world-behind-the-world, but she could not think of anything that made her a valuable resource to Caledonia, or to the worldwide Fae Interpol.

***

Leah's feet were up on the table as she leaned back, drinking her tea. The manual was in her other hand, and she was laughing quietly to herself as she read through it.

Chief Ben pushed her feet off the desk. Startled, she set down her mug.

"Working hard, I see?" he asked.

"Sorry, Chief," she said.

Dorian walked in and nodded to them.

"I need you both to go down to the Britannia Panopticon," said Ben. "There's been a report of a haunting."

"A haunting at the Britannia Panopticon," said Dorian, "How novel."

"You can put that sarcasm back where you found it, Dorian," said the Chief. "Let's get a move on."

"We've already got a case," said Leah.

Chief Ben gave her a look she could only classify as the promise of encroaching unemployment.

"Yes, and Glasgow grinds to a halt while your investigation is going on?" he said. "You're still police officers, and everyone else is busy. Off you go."

He ambled over to his desk and disappeared behind the stacks of paperwork that only ever seemed to grow.

Leah reluctantly set down her manual, and followed Dorian into the cool evening, the sky littered with stars.

***

The Britannia Panopticon was a music hall built many years earlier. It still hosted vaudeville acts from time to time. Outside of the building, a dapper man dressed in Victorian clothing advertised upcoming shows, calling out to the passing crowds like a carnival barker.

"Maybe you should apply for this job," Leah said to Dorian. "You might make some spending money."

"Indeed?" asked Dorian. "And what do I need spending money for?"

"You could buy a new waistcoat?" Leah suggested.

"These are custom-made in Italy by my own tailor," sniffed Dorian. "Magnus and I have been alive for centuries. We made wise investments."

Leah didn't know what to say.

"Oh," she said, and thought of the previous week, when she had counted out her change, embarrassed, just to buy a bottle to get her through the night. The Greys would never understand.

Dorian, as usual, could hear her thoughts.

"We were lucky," he said. "There are many Fae who were not so responsible with human money. Faerie gold is useless in this world."

"Trying to make me feel better?" she asked. "I've been broke for years. I hope Caledonia doesn't pay in Fae gold."

Dorian smiled.

"No," he said, "it pays in Scottish pounds. Good benefits, too. They realise what risks we are all taking - you, Leah, more than any of us."

"Great," she said. "You fill me with confidence."

They arrived at the Panopticon's door. They went inside, and it shut behind them. The dusty, cavernous theatre was dark and forbidding. Leah was a bit taken aback.

It was quiet. Motes of dust floated through sunlight slanting through the huge, empty space. Tiny orbs glowed for a moment, turning slowly as they drifted across the hall, and then vanished.

"What are those?" she asked.

"Ghosts," Dorian said.

He sighed and smiled. She looked at him sideways.

"Ghosts of an earlier time," he explained. "The Victorian era, and before. They are happy. They can still see the shows playing."

Leah stared up at the orbs, spinning slowly through the room.

"Ghost orbs," she said, "watching ghost plays? How can there be a ghost play?"

"There are ghost versions of just about everything," he said. "Many ghosts are in an existential loop, one aspect of their lives repeating again and again. The orbs are the happiest of spirits, because they inhabit a world of pleasant things. This music hall is also haunted by the excitement of opening night, the chance of spotting a celebrity, and the butterfly sensations just before actors take the stage. Many buildings and places are haunted primarily by an emotion, and the Britannia Panopticon is one of the buildings whose primary emotion is happiness."

"Wow," said Leah, and meant it. She realised that for Dorian, a creature who could sense emotion and read thoughts, the emotion of things and places must be quite overwhelming. It would be calming to be in an environment like the Britannia Panopticon.

"Unfortunately," he said, "there are a few restless spirits here. I know about the chimp but I don't know why it is misbehaving suddenly."

"Tell me about it," said Leah. "The world's oldest surviving music hall must have plenty of stories."

"You know," said Dorian, "that somewhere, all stories are true."

Leah raised an eyebrow.

"And that all stories have power," he added.

"Stories have always held fascination for people worldwide," she agreed. "But until I started working for Caledonia, I hadn't realised that stories had a *literal* power. What's the story here?"

"Years ago, the Britannia Panopticon housed a zoo," said Dorian. "One of the creatures in it, a chimpanzee named Solomon, also known as Solomon the Man Monkey, is said to haunt the building."

"*Is said to?*" Leah repeated. "You mean you don't know?"

Dorian shook his head.

"We are familiar with many characters in the city," he said. "But we do not know them all, nor do we necessarily have proof of their existence."

"But you said stories have power," said Leah. "Doesn't that mean that it becomes true, whether or not it was real?"

"It depends on the story," said Dorian. "Ghosts, for example, have to have been living beings first. While storytelling can create monsters, not everything will come into being every time. So that means - "

"If there is a chimp here, it was a real animal once?" Leah asked.

Dorian nodded.

Suddenly, the dust motes began to dance excitedly. Leah and Dorian looked at each other. They threw themselves out of the way as something invisible came barrelling through where they had been standing, leaving huge footprints on the dusty floor. Catching her breath, Leah stood up. She looked at the prints - large knuckles and feet.

"So," she paused. "Real, then?"

"Yes," said Dorian, and they moved aside quickly to avoid the second pass.

"What do we do?" shouted Leah.

"I don't know, Miss Bishop!" he shouted back. "This is as far as I've ever gotten!"

Leah rolled her eyes.

"Oh, useless!" she said. "Can't you start a tornado or something?"

"Weather does not exist indoors!" Dorian said.

Leah could feel the floor shaking beneath her feet as the chimpanzee charged. She shut her eyes against the upcoming collision, but she did not move. Dorian hid his face.

There was silence, and the soft whuffling of an animal sniffing. Dorian raised his head in astonishment.

Leah opened her eyes. She saw nothing but she could feel the hot breath and smell the menagerie scent of the ape. She felt a huge hand pat her head, and to her surprise, take something out of her pocket. She felt another cool, leathery hand gently unfold her fingers, so her hand was held out, palm upraised. A packet of tea dropped onto her open palm. Scottish Breakfast. Leah looked at the packet, and up toward the empty space where the chimpanzee's head would be.

Dorian raised one perfect eyebrow.

"I think," she whispered, "that it wants me to make tea."

Dorian sat up.

"What?" he asked.

She showed him the packet. The chimpanzee whuffled again, waiting patiently.

"I think I should make it tea," she whispered. "Where is the kettle? Does the building have one?"

"Yes," said Dorian. "It's still in use, so... the kitchen?"

"Which way?"

"Over there."

Leah backed slowly out of the room and went into the kitchen. Dorian sat with the chimpanzee. It hadn't moved, but he could hear its steady breathing.

Leah returned with a teacup and saucer.

"How is it going to drink from that?!" Dorian hissed. "It's a chimpanzee."

It was too late. Solomon had taken the cup and saucer from

her. To their disbelief, they watched as the cup was lifted by something invisible, and the tea drained into nothingness.

"Do you think its pinkie finger is out?" whispered Leah.

"Ssshhh!" Dorian whispered back.

The tea finished, the cup was set back into the saucer, and placed onto the floor. There was a rumbling noise of animal approval, and the presence faded. The theatre was filled once again with the motes of dust and the light orbs that wheeled in a slow dance across the ceiling.

"What was that about?" asked Dorian.

"Well," said Leah, "the chimp *was* British, after all."

***

Upon reporting back to the station, Chief Ben nodded sagely.

"We will have to appoint someone to go there on occasion and bring tea," he said. "Eternity without tea would be unthinkable, and we would be guilty of abuse if we did not provide it."

Dorian nodded in agreement, as if this truth was self-evident. Leah looked at the two men and shook her head.

"Looks like we're back to the paperwork," sighed Dorian.

"Seems that way," Leah replied.

***

After a few hours, they were both quite bored. Leah rubbed her eyes and looked over at her partner. She was ready to take a break.

"So," said Leah. "What is the story behind Cuchulainn? I was under the impression that it was Finn MacCool he fought. I went and looked it up but I couldn't find any mention of Benandonner and Cuchulainn in any of our folklore portals."

Dorian smiled.

"I think it's best if the Chief tells you," he said. "I wasn't there, of course, and the tale grows in the telling. Stories are dangerous."

Dorian disappeared behind the stacks and emerged a few minutes later. Grumbling, Chief Ben walked out and sat down with them.

"Folklorists," he said. "Always getting it wrong! The only story that has lasted is the story where I am a coward! There were many giants then."

"And ghost giants," said Leah. "Or so I've heard."

"Yes," he said. "We once numbered in the thousands. Not everyone is still alive, of course, but some of them are still here, as ghosts, if they did not make it to the other side."

Leah sat down with her tea. Ben eyed the two of them.

"You know, there is a lot of work to do," he said. "That paperwork won't do itself."

"Oh, go on, Chief," said Leah. "You can take a break. Besides, I *am* a folklorist. Maybe I can help you set the story straight."

"Unlikely," he said. "As you're a police officer now, and you've only got my word for it. Even so. They were right about me and Finn MacCool. Not one of my proudest moments."

He studied the tall window on the opposite side of the room, filling the library with the greylight of Glasgow.

"And the Causeway is still there, every day reminding me of my one act of cowardice," he sighed. "I was much younger then, hotheaded. Stupid, really. How could I not have known that was Finn himself there, in the crib? He built the Causeway so I could fight him, and then I was tricked by him and his wife, destroying the bridge between Antrim and Scotland as I ran back here in terror. How everyone laughed, when the truth came out.

'I endeavoured to prove everyone wrong after that. Of course I heard the story had travelled throughout the Highlands, bringing great amusement to Fae and human alike. I wanted to show them that I was no coward and no fool. And what better way to do that than to fight the ultimate giant? Cuchulainn, the great hero of the Ulster cycle, as they call it today.

'So, I travelled. I went beneath the sea, and I walked along the seabed, all the way to Skye. He had trained with the great warrior-woman, Scathach. Now there was a woman you did not want to meet! A lion's mane of red hair and blazing green eyes. She was more terrifying than any monster or creature before or since. Sadly, Scathach was a human, and has long since passed out of this world. Many times, the Fae still visit her grave to pay their respects.

'The fame of Cuchulainn had reached the ears of every human and Fae in these islands by that time. I encountered him in the centre of Skye. We fought such a mighty battle! The earth shook, and burst beneath our tramping feet! The crash of our clubs, the slash of our swords! And then Cuchulainn missed, and his great sword sliced too deep into the earth. Water sprang up, blue like dreams. It rushed to fill in the cracks made by the weapon. I took him down, and his great body cracked the earth further. Near to drowning, Cuchulainn begged me to save him. I wanted the victory, and yet I reached out my hand. I lifted him up, and there our friendship was forged. Those waters were blessed then, and now. The curse of evil and the blessing of good. The two Fae states of being, together.

'They say if you swim there, in the Fairy Pools of Skye, the Fae might steal your soul. And we might. But other tales are told, of healing and of magic. A meeting begun in war, ended in friendship. They are beautiful, the Fairy Pools, and treacherous, because the Fae created them. The humans that visit are captivated, but they also take their chances."

Leah was grinning from ear to ear.

"That's magnificent!" she cried happily. "What a wonderful story!"

Benandonner nodded, smiling himself.

"Ah, yes," he said. "I might have joined the pantheon, with the other gods and giants. And yet, for some reason, this story did not reach the ears of everyone - but my act of cowardice with Finn MacCool did. Although I remained friends with Cuchulainn, this event passed from memory without even becoming myth.

'So, I began my life's work, with this branch of the Fae police.

Here is where I plan to leave my legacy. A myth borne of hard work and dedication, a story that may never reach human ears. But all the Fae now know my name is associated with something other than an ancient tale of destruction and cowardice."

"If you would permit me to suggest something," said Dorian politely, and Ben nodded. "Human ears have heard the tale now."

He gestured toward Leah, and Chief Ben leaned back in his chair, smiling. This seemed to have been all he had ever wanted, to be known as the hero he had become, rather than the foolish villain in faerie tales. Leah smiled.

"I will be sure to start telling the story," she assured her boss. The chief nodded a gruff thanks.

Dorian looked at her with an indescribable expression.

"Do that, Leah," he said. "But always remember - stories are dangerous, and they can take on a life of their own."

Leah nodded, a bit perplexed.

"You keep saying things like *stories are dangerous,*" she confronted him. "What do you mean?"

Dorian favoured her with a half-smile.

"You are inquisitive," he said. "But of course you are, as a researcher."

He turned in his chair.

"We - the supernaturals - we are the story," he began. "You - humanity - you are the storytellers, the world-weavers. Not every story comes true, but those tales forged in pain and blood, those believed with the heart and soul, those legends become reality, somewhere."

Leah's eyes grew large.

"You mean..." she said quietly. "Everything humans think of is real? Everything?"

Dorian shook his head.

"Not every thought that crosses your minds," he replied. "Not everything you scribble absentmindedly on a page. Those stories which ignite and spread like wildfire, or those which are born of terrible suffering, become our reality. There is power in *being* the story: limitless magic, keys that fit locks leading to other worlds, secret green fairy rings and hollows in the hills, but in the end, the real power lies with the storyteller."

Dorian's voice changed. There was some undercurrent, dark and powerful. Leah sensed that there was a truth in it, threatening to pull her under.

"Think on this, when you tell the tale. Think on this, when you discover a new passion, a new fear developing in the hearts and minds of man: all monsters had to come from somewhere," said Dorian Grey.

Chapter Eight

Dylan sat beside Tearlach as they waited for the police. He returned to the morning's conversation.

"D'you play any fitba?" he asked.

Tearlach had found the chips and curry that one of the officers had left for the two of them and hesitantly tried it. He tried it again. Since he wasn't entirely certain he decided to try it one more time.

"Football?" he asked absentmindedly, staring raptly at the food. "What's that?"

Dylan turned to his friend in disbelief.

"*Wit's tha'*? *Wit's tha'*?" he said.

Tearlach stared at him with round eyes, a chip halfway to his mouth.

Dylan pointed at the chip and shouted, "*WIT'S THA'*?!"

"*You give tha' here the noo, Tearlach,*" he said.

He snatched the food out of Tearlach's hands. Tearlach grabbed for it, and missed.

"What for?" Tearlach complained.

Dylan collared a passing officer and shoved the polystyrene box into their hands.

"You cannae be giein' him this rubbish!" Dylan admonished the officer. "He's a *Highlander*. Get him lamb and mash! He's gonna get ill!"

As Dylan harangued the officer, Tearlach spied the unopened can of Irn-Bru on the desk.

"Ooh," he said, just as Dylan caught sight of what he was after.

"*No Tearlach you cannae ha' the Irn-Bru, you get back here right now*!" Dylan shouted. Tearlach leaped off the desk, kilt flying, and made tracks down the hallway with Dylan in hot pursuit.

**

Leah opened the door just after they left. She walked up to Dorian who was sitting in front of the murder board, drinking his tea in a contemplative fashion. He kept staring at every face in turn, shaking his head. He couldn't seem to make heads or tails of any of it. He caught sight of Leah.

"Oh, good," he said. "I was lost in *ennui*."

"Have you seen Magnus?" she asked.

"Not lately," he said. "Why?"

"He-" she began, and then saw the door open. "Never mind, they're back again."

Dylan had apprehended the can of Irn-Bru from Tearlach, and walked straight up to Dorian, incensed. He shook a finger in Dorian's face.

"Whit do ye think yir daein'?" he demanded. "Feedin' him this? He needs good, nourishin', healthy food! We can live on this, but he cannae!"

Dorian held his gaze, effortlessly, as befit a man who could have brought a nation to its knees with a disapproving stare.

"You lower your voice, young man, or I'm confiscating your Highlander," he said.

Dylan rose to his full height.

"*You wit*?" Dylan said. "I know the polis, and yir polis, no matter what kinda polis y'are. An' you dinnae ha' the time to be takin' care of Tearlach. I do. I found him. I'm responsible, so I am."

Tearlach had had enough of this, and set down the chips he had started to eat again. He went up to Dylan, his countenance darkened.

"Look here, I am not your pet!" Tearlach said.

"But yir ma responsibility," Dylan said firmly. "I will watch out for you until we can get you hame an' awa' from this filth."

Tearlach looked around the room, unsure what Dylan was

74

referring to.

"May I please have some of that orange ambrosia?" asked Tearlach, pointing at the can. Dylan's eyes narrowed.

"Nae, you may no'," he said firmly, and glared at Dorian, who shrugged.

***

It turned out that Magnus had been in the kitchen, hiding from his overdue paperwork. He and Dorian were discussing the case when Leah joined them. She decided to try the coffee again, and poured out some of the blackest slop she had ever seen into a mug that said *#1 Boss!*

She realised it must belong to Chief Ben. She wondered who had given it to him.

"Well, that's that," said Dorian. "This one goes back to the real-world police."

"What? Why?" asked Leah. "I thought Milo said he'd never seen anything like it."

"The tests are notoriously unreliable," said Magnus. "It's probably a coincidence. Anyway, that makes the killer definitively human - even if he *has* been killing the Fae. Either he is aware of our existence, or it is another coincidence."

"That's a lot of coincidences," said Leah.

"Yes," agreed Dorian. "But if the tests are giving us ridiculous answers, then it's probably human. The genes were human and so the police get the case."

Leah grimaced. This was one of her more recent attempts to understand why people seemed to like coffee so much, and she still didn't see the attraction. Dorian drank his espresso with apparent enjoyment, mystifying her.

"I'm sorry," said Leah. "But... what if the tests are correct? What if there really is some kind of new creature out there systematically killing off the Fae?"

"It's possible," said Magnus. "But unlikely. That would be a wild and incredible thing, wouldn't it? Too often we think a case is ours, and it turns out we've been barking up the wrong tree, so to speak. Besides, the Fae are traditionalists. It's one of the reasons this idiot gets away with dressing like he does. You're stuck in the era you were Taken."

Magnus, giving Dorian a significant look, picked up his mug and walked out if the kitchen.

"Don't listen to him," said Dorian. "He's just disappointed that he's not been Taken yet."

Leah stared at him.

"Why would he be disappointed?" she asked. "He gets laid every single night, quite easily. That sounds like a dream come true, for some people."

Dorian grinned.

"For humans... maybe. A selkie's fondest wish is to be Taken, to fall in love."

"Doesn't seem like it's done you any good," Leah said.

"On the contrary," said Dorian. "She remains all I live for, and for a selkie, a life spent in love means a life well lived. Selkies like Magnus consider their lives wasted. It's fine for our youth, to find ourselves with many people, of course, many selkies are like humans in that way, but Magnus is far past his sell-by date."

"He looks the same age as you," Leah said.

"Perhaps," said Dorian. "But not to me. Selkies can see the true age of other seal-people, and Magnus is an old, old man. Love grants true youth to the selk. We are indeed like vampires, but we are a race that feeds on love instead of blood."

This thought seemed to have just occurred to him, and he made a *moue* of distaste.

"Your woman. You knew her when?" Leah asked.

"During the Victorian era, as Magnus says," he replied. "I met her in 1896. In Paris, which might please the romantic in you. It was the height of the Bohemian era, one of those beautiful moments in history. The Fae always know those times will only last for a moment, because we've seen them all before. It seems that the default for this world is darkness or boredom. Those bright moments in history are like the Fae world bleeding into this one, for a while. Those times of light are more striking, like a match that will soon burn out, and we are drawn to them, just as humans are. There is a reason they called it the *Belle Époque*, but it was only one of many. There were times like it before, there will be times like it again. Not always in the same city, or the same country. The *beautiful age* can happen anywhere. Still, it was a poignant time to be in love."

He sighed, faraway.

"So... she must have passed away, then?" Leah asked.

Dorian started and came back to himself.

"Yes," said Dorian. "I felt her going. Her soul was linked to mine, though mine was no longer to hers."

He paused, trying to compose himself. Leah was surprised to recognise that he was holding back tears, his long black lashes blinking them away. He finally spoke again.

"It was a dreadful day."

Leah stared at him, speechless for a moment.

"Even though she's passed on... you are still not free?" she finally said. He looked at her, almost affronted.

"Free? You assume that such freedom would be a blessing. Not for me, and not for any selkie. If she had remained with me, I would have truly loved her throughout her old age. For much like we look young to you, you will always appear young and beautiful to us. There is no difference."

Leah shook her head.

"Humans think they truly love," she said. "Seems that we are wrong."

Dorian looked at her with a serious expression.

"I feel your pain," he said. "I mean that truly. I can hear it, in your heartbeat, and see it in the cast of your soul like a shadow. It is what selkies were made to do. In your feelings of loss, humans differ from selkies. Though our love remains permanent, the loss does not hurt us the way it does you. I do not envy you your humanity."

"How long was she with you? Before she left?" Leah asked.

Dorian smiled.

"Three years, two months, four days, ten hours, twenty minutes, and thirty-seven seconds," he said. "But I was, for her, only a respite, and not the cure that she needed. She found that in another man, a human like yourself. She stayed with him until his death, and died four years afterwards."

"So... you have spent the last... century in love with a woman who was only with you for a few years?" Leah asked.

"It could have been worse," said Dorian. "I could still remain Untaken, like Magnus. As it was, I was getting a bit long in the tooth when she called me. The world has not improved much since those days. I expect another beautiful age to occur soon, somewhere on the planet. When it does, I will request a transfer from the chief."

Leah shook her head.

Her thoughts were of Paris and Montmartre, cosy little cafés and a love long since dead. The stars of Paris, they shine on, she thought, they shine today like they did then, like a Fae's love for a human. Human love, so impermanent, so inconstant, thrown away on a whim, like a laugh in a crowd or a dropped handkerchief, leaving the shadowed silhouette of this Victorian beauty, lost to time, walking broken and eternal, down the centuries alone.

She nearly wept for him then, for she knew loneliness. Compounded by centuries, it was an impossible thought. She slowly returned to the present day. A thought had been bothering her, an irritating grain of sand, the inside sunset of a shining clamshell, something just out of her reach. An idea, perhaps a pearl.

"Something about this still doesn't sit well with me, Dorian," said Leah. "Something about this case, I mean. I just don't believe the answer is as simple as a human killer, although I never thought I would hear myself say something like that. There's something else going on here, I can feel it."

"I understand -" Dorian began, and then turned towards the door as it opened.

Glorious light streamed into the station, illuminating every corner. Standing in the centre of this light, striding forward, was a vision; a fairytale prince. He had strange and wild green eyes, set back in his skull, with prominent cheekbones in a pale face. He was handsome and strong, ensconced in a momentary corona as if the light lived only to serve him. Leah was startled when Dorian bowed deeply to him, almost genuflecting.

The man was breathtaking, his presence commanding and surreal.

"Sebastian is your killer," he announced. "I know... because it's my fault."

Chapter Nine

onghas stood in the shadows near the doorway, holding the slip of paper between his fingers in disgust. The world was dark there, and he saw only the vague outline of a man standing against tall windows, a silhouette in the setting sun. The light that Aonghas could emanate, his eyes glowing, was dull, as if something had snuffed it out.

"I am glad you decided to join me," said a slithering voice.

The Trooping Faerie refused to move.

"What do you want from me, Sebastian?" he asked.

"Many years ago," said the voice, "I saved you from a foolish mistake."

"Yes," said Aonghas. "I remember."

Sebastian paced the floor.

"Glasgow needed protecting," he said. "You had already been gone too long as it was. If you had been captured, the west winds would have been open to enemies. As you know, a Guardian is only called after the former Guardian dies. They would have imprisoned, rather than killed, you. The city would have been vulnerable."

Aonghas nodded.

"I thank you for your help," said Aonghas. "It was stupid of me, and I have not done it since. You sent me this message to remind me of my debt. What do you want of me?"

Sebastian poured himself a whisky.

"Why don't you join me?" he asked, motioning to an empty seat next to him. "You can have a drink if you like. I am well aware of your... temptations."

"I prefer to stand," said Aonghas stiffly, but the hunger was there all the same as he watched Sebastian decant the amber liquid into a glass.

"Suit yourself," said Sebastian. *"I require your services. Or rather, for you and the other Guardians to look the other way, just this once."*

"What do you plan to do?"

"It is already done. The Fae have perished. The police are lost. I'd like to keep it that way."

Aonghas felt every hair on his body stand on end.

"You are behind the killings?" he asked. *"You? I never saw you as a killer, Sebastian. A thief, a criminal, a mobster - not a killer."*

"Don't worry," said Sebastian in a soothing voice. *"It will be over soon. I am nearing my goal as we speak."*

Aonghas felt ill. He put a hand against the wall to steady himself.

"You could be next, Aonghas," said Sebastian. *"I need you to do this for me. Then your debt is paid."*

"I have looked away from your crimes for too long, Sebastian," he said. *"And you have gone too far, this time. To what end, I cannot fathom; all I know is that innocent Fae have lost their lives."*

Aonghas straightened, standing tall and menacing. It was time for him to take responsibility, and once again, serve his purpose.

"I am a Guardian of Glasgow," he said in a voice of hardened steel woven with concrete, broken fences, abandoned lots, and lost dreams.

Sebastian set down his glass with a clink. He stood up and approached the Trooping Faerie.

"You, a Guardian of Glasgow?!" he laughed. *"A drunken, useless Elf constantly bitching about the good old days? I'm sorry. I am mistaken. You're not an Elf any longer. You're barely even a man. You have not deserved your title in many, many years."*

Aonghas stood his ground. His eyes glowed softly white, and lightning began to crackle from his fingertips.

"Perhaps I have been remiss in my duties," he said. *"But the power has never left me. It is time I wore this mantle properly. What can you do against me, Sebastian? You are just a man."*

Sebastian flung photographs from the crime scenes at Aonghas's feet. Dead faeries gazed up at him, bloodless and pale.

"I have power you cannot imagine," he said. "You have made your choice, and you betray me."

Aonghas nodded.

"Yes," he said. "I do."

He turned to leave.

"I certainly hope you realise that your choice will have... consequences," said Sebastian.

"I'm counting on it," said Aonghas, and he walked outside, trying not to show the terror he felt.

In the rain and wind of a hazy Glasgow afternoon, Aonghas walked through the streets against the gale that was building. He could feel his heart beating wildly in his chest. He knew who the serial killer was, and had information the police could use to catch him. He knew also that Sebastian had somehow acquired enough power to destroy the immortal. Most of them could not be killed by any means.

He paused a moment, before a green pavilion, in a rough neighbourhood of the city. There were many entrances to Caledonia Interpol; anything that looked incongruous and beautiful in the city was often a portal to the office. Police officers in trouble would run towards anything that looked out of place, and this beautiful wrought-iron pavilion clearly did not belong.

Aonghas placed a palm flat against one of the pillars, and looked up at the structure, an architectural gem, a thought and memory of his world, his home. Both he and the pavilion, desperately beautiful, desperately alone. He stepped inside, and let the magic take him.

He stood at the entrance of Caledonia Interpol, weighing his options. He made his decision, sighed, and pushed the door open.

***

"That was very dramatic," Leah whispered to Dorian, who shushed her.

"He is still an Elf," he said. "He has to tell the story his way." To Aonghas he said, "Go on, my lord. What happened? Why do

83

you owe Sebastian this debt?"

"I went on holiday," said Aonghas.

"*What?*"

"I was tired, Dorian. I wanted to take some time off, and I went to Dublin. I hadn't been to Ireland since Ninian's time, and it has changed vastly."

He caught a glimpse of his reflection in the window, how pale he looked, haggard and drawn.

"I must admit, so have I," he said. "Once, I would certainly have tempted the loveliest of the village ladies to my silver bower."

He looked at Leah significantly, and she snorted. He sighed, and stared down at himself.

"But now - I do not know if it is the influence of Glasgow's modern culture or not - I have had to be satisfied with just about anything."

"Aonghas," said Dorian. "What happened in Dublin?"

Dublin, Republic of Ireland

The pub in Temple Bar was serving up its last round. Aonghas enjoyed the company of the Irish; the way they surrounded a newcomer and bought him all the alcohol he could possibly desire, and probably more.

In the warm wine glow of the pub, Aonghas was laughing without a care in the world. He was unbelievably happy and hadn't felt such a weight off his chest in centuries. He didn't usually take holidays from his guarding place in Glasgow, but this was only for an evening. His companions were brilliant, intellectual young gentlemen - or so they had seemed through his whisky haze.

He felt the cold of the handcuffs before they had trapped him in them - iron. True binding for the Fae, who could get out of almost anything. Aonghas groaned. The Dublin Fae Police. The Glasgow branch he had to deal with was bad enough.

"A bit out of your jurisdiction, aren't you, Aonghas Mòr?" snarled the police officer in his ear.

❧ CHAPTER NINE ❧

"What about you? Gone off chasing lonely travellers?" Aonghas replied to the dullahan who had him tied. Its horrific visage grinned out at him from under the creature's arm. The dullahan were headless horsemen who used human spines for whips and carried their heads in the crook of their elbows. Aonghas was surprised, as generally only Seelie Court faeries were allowed on the UK or Ireland forces. Perhaps this dullahan was reformed. But only just, he discovered, as he was thrown to the ground.

"Is there a problem here, officers?" asked one of the men he'd been drinking with. His smile revealed a gold tooth. Aonghas groaned. His night was about to get worse. Leprechauns were the macho type and they didn't really hold with pretty Trooping Faerie men, neds or no. Had he known he was drinking with leprechauns he'd have run a mile. The police could put him in jail for 1,000 years - the average punishment for going AWOL.

Leprechauns could, would, and indeed had, tortured him for a time-without-time, as they could bend time into a Möbius strip and do as they pleased. Pots of gold were just a side thing, essentially their bank accounts.

And then the strangest thing happened. The leprechauns attacked the dullahan, forcing him down onto the floor. Aonghas gaped at them in disbelief. One of the leprechauns sitting on top of the police officer looked at him.

"Remember this, Aonghas," he said. "Remember what our boss has done for you tonight."

Aonghas looked around the pub.

"Sebastian," said the leprechaun. "He isn't fool enough to show his face here. Remember his name. He will remind you of this incident, when he needs you. Be quick to come when you are called. Now get out of here! Before more of them show up."

Aonghas didn't need to be told twice. He didn't much care for the police, but they were the least of his worries now.

He had learned to fear Sebastian long ago.

***

"Sounds t'me like you dinnae deserve your job," Dylan interjected.

Dorian and Leah were startled. They had quite forgotten that Dylan and Tearlach were there.

Aonghas turned to look at him in slow astonishment. How could this young upstart ned have anything to say about the ancient Fae and their problems?

Dylan crossed his arms, and looked at Dorian and Leah in defiance.

"Well? He's meant t'watch o'er Glesga, an he wandered off tae get pissed on holiday! You do tha' at any job, you get the sack! Who knows what coulda happened? Hell, look what *has* happened!"

"Who knows, indeed," Dorian agreed. "Aonghas, what were you thinking?"

But Aonghas was staring with something akin to amusement at Dylan, who glared at the Trooping Faerie.

Dorian looked from the one to the other.

"He doesn't know, does he?" Aonghas asked.

Dorian shook his head slightly.

"I don't think that now is the time, Aonghas," Dorian said.

This exchange was not lost on Dylan.

"I dinnae ken what?" he demanded.

He looked to Tearlach for support, but his friend shrugged.

"You are Fae," said Aonghas, and smiled smugly. Dorian sighed.

"Aonghas-"

"Wit does tha' mean?" he asked.

He looked at Leah, then Dorian, then Tearlach.

Tearlach put his arm around his friend's shoulder, grinning.

"It means that you're a faerie, Dylan," Tearlach said, bursting with pride.

"Get tae fuck," said Dylan. "So's yer maw!"

"He means you're a faerie," said Leah. "An actual faerie."

Dylan stared.

"Wit... like... wi' wings an all?" he stuttered.

"If you like," said Aonghas. "I have them."

There was a blinding white light.

The sound of hearts beating.

Dylan fell to his knees, and the skin of his back split along his shoulder blades. He cried out, as blood-streaked feathers emerged, the arch of two white wings. He sobbed in exquisite agony as the great wings pushed free, and spread out in a sound of wind and blood. The skin of his back healed instantly, the only proof of their birth the blood streaming from the feathers. He wiped the tears from his face, ashamed. Dylan got to his feet, drained from the experience, as the huge wings stretched out across the room. They dwarfed him, and he shook them out, trying a few tremulous beats, cautiously newborn, testing the air.

"That's not a faerie. That's an angel!" cried Leah.

Aonghas grinned.

"And aren't we all," he said. "There you go, Dylan. A ned angel."

"I cannae be an angel! I nick things!" Dylan said, trying to manoeuvre with the enormous wings.

"You *are* a faerie," said Aonghas. "Your imagination manifested these wings."

Dylan crossed his arms again and nearly fell over from the weight of the wings.

"How do I... put these away?" he demanded. "Let's see yirs!"

Aonghas's dragonfly-rainbow wings fluttered out, and the two Trooping Faeries stared at each other. They were like a strange mirror image; both had shaved heads, one with delicate, transparent glittering wings and the other with soft white feathered wings that overshadowed him and the room. One wore a Rangers hoodie, the other was in a Celtic tracksuit with a shamrock tattoo on his neck.

Leah smiled at this.

"Only in Glasgow," she said, and shook her head.

"Aonghas," said Dorian. "If Dylan has been called, then that means - "

"Yes," agreed Aonghas. "One of the Guardians is dead. And Dylan has been called to replace him."

"This must be the reason that Tearlach ended up on Sauchiehall Street," said Dorian. "Dylan wouldn't realise it, of course, but Trooping Faeries control time. Even dreaming, for them, is dangerous - being drunk, even more."

Dylan pushed some of the huge feathers aside to peer with violence at Dorian.

"You tellin' me I cannae drink anymair?" said Dylan.

"It would be unwise," said Dorian primly, arranging his gloves.

"How dae we get Tearlach back hame?" asked Dylan. "Someone aroun' here needs t'be responsible, an' it seems t'be ma fault he wound up here."

"You are the strangest ned I have ever met," said Leah.

Dylan just glared. He indicated the food they had provided for Tearlach.

"Widjae get him su'n mair appropriate, lamb an' mash, or su'n?" he said.

Leah and Dorian exchanged glances.

"I am a grown man, Dylan," said Tearlach.

"Aye, we can see tha', wi' all yir muscles rippling all over everywhere," Dylan retorted. "It doesnae mean tha' you should be eatin' this."

"Hmm," mused Dorian.

He looked at Leah, who nodded.

"Maybe you should go back in time with him," suggested Leah.

Dylan goggled at them.

"Wit?" he asked. "What guid would tha' do? An' can someone help me put these things away already?!"

Aonghas laughed and touched a wingtip. They vanished.

"Just takes practice," he said. "You'll get used to it. Although I wouldn't recommend bringing them out in a small room."

"Yes, Dylan, come back with me," said Tearlach. "You certainly don't seem to like it in this day and age."

❀ CHAPTER NINE ❀

"Oh, aye?" he said. "But wha's in charge a Glesga then? Wha's in charge o' my city, my people? This numptie? He *abandoned* Glesga, he abandoned us."

Dorian gave Dylan a warning look.

"Dylan, Aonghas is a High Faerie," said Dorian. "He out-ranks us all - "

"Aye?" said Dylan, rounding on the selkie, "Wull, he's certainly been high, all right! I may no' be ancient, but I m a better man than him."

Aonghas opened his mouth. Dylan's white wings manifested with a snap, like a sail filling with wind.

"Nae," said Dylan, shaking his finger in Aonghas's face. "Nae. Don' you dare. *Don' you dare.*"

Tearlach stood and went to Dylan, whose wings vibrated with emotion.

"*Where was he*, when *ma mum died* of an overdose?!" Dylan shouted. "*Where was he*, when I had tae take care of ma wee sister? I was alone, an' he went on holiday!"

Tearlach took his hand.

"Ma wee sister is deid," said Dylan. "Ma mum is deid. I was six. Ma mum died in the street, an' she told me the government would come an' separate us. She said they would put us in a horrible place where we'd be tortured an' abused. I didnae ken how to take care of a wee bairn. I tried t'gie her food, an' milk, an' she died in my arms, Aonghas. Ma sister died in ma arms, and I was too afraid to ask for help, so I was. *I was six years old.*"

He held Aonghas's gaze.

"I was a smart bairn," he went on. "I widnae deal drugs, an' I wanted tae make something of masel'. I stole books. I begged on street corners. I read. I fought, I made friends, I lost them. I enrolled masel' in school. They never asked. *They never once asked where ma mother was.*"

Dylan turned, his wings spread wide.

"Wi' all yir talk of neds, an' yir superiority - aye, I *am* a ned. An' proud of it. I wisnae raised, *I was forged.*"

Dylan went up to Aonghas, and put his face very close to the

Fae. He looked into his eyes.

"So I am asking you again, Aonghas Mòr, Guardian of Glesga," said Dylan. *"Where ha' you been?"*

Everyone in the room was silent. Aonghas stared at the ground. Tearlach's expression was dark and tears brimmed in his eyes.

"He asked you a question," said Tearlach, and the clear hardness of his voice rang out with the memory of war and loss. The Highland warrior in him was evident in every sinew, flecks of iron in every word.

Aonghas shrugged. None of this had an effect on him. He had been around too long, and had seen too much. He did not feel responsible, not for the state of the city nor for these young and foolish creatures stupid enough to defy him. He was a powerful Trooping Faerie, from the days when there had been no city here. He was eternal, and he no longer much cared what people thought of him.

"He's right," he said. "I am not the Fae for the job. That doesn't matter, it's still mine. I cannot give it up, and it is not my responsibility what happens to individual Glaswegians."

Dylan gave him an incredulous look.

"Oh, aye?" he demanded. "Wull, tha's no' how it works, the way I see it. If yir magic, if you hae power, if yir giein su'n t'do, you oughta bloody well do it. If a place needs protection, it's yir job t'mak' sure that the place is protected."

"Aye," said Tearlach. "You are an all-powerful Fae. You have no excuse. Even the children of my clan are warriors, and they have nothing but their own bravery to guide them."

Both Dorian and Leah were surprised by Dylan's outburst, but Tearlach was proud, as if he'd always known that Dylan was capable of this sort of selfless loyalty.

Dylan managed to fold in his wings, throw the doors open, and go outside. Tearlach looked around the room with a gaze like thunder, and then followed him out the door.

Chapter Ten

This certainly explains a great deal," said Dorian. "Irresponsible isn't the word, Aonghas. You have much to answer for - to Dylan first of all, and then to the Fae Council."

Aonghas blanched.

"You... you wouldn't put the Fae Council on me for this?" he asked.

Dorian ignored him, turning instead to Leah.

"Aonghas claims he was gone for *an evening*," said Dorian witheringly. "But you're a folklorist, Leah. Tell me how long *an evening* is."

"Well," said Leah, thinking, "in the Fairy Reel story of the two brothers, one stayed to dance and the other went home. The brother who danced - it was some weeks before he even completed the first reel, months went past, and years even... "

She turned slowly to look at Aonghas.

"You were gone... *for years*?" she asked.

"There are other Guardians!" Aonghas said defensively, holding his hands up. "They're responsible too."

"And how many of them, do you think, now owe a favour to this Sebastian?" asked Leah.

Aonghas closed his mouth.

"Leaving the city means leaving one edge of it open," explained Dorian. "A tear in the cloth. Even if the other Guardians were vigilant, they face outwards. Once danger is within the city walls, so to speak, it is more difficult to sense. *Anything* could be out there now, Aonghas. Anything at all."

Leah had been silent while they spoke. She looked up.

"So... " she said. "The shipping industry goes under. Poverty. Drugs. This has been a hard city since the beginning, but it was working-class hard. Are you telling me it's like this now because you wanted to go to a *bar*?"

The storm in Dorian's expression was unmistakable.

Aonghas did not reply.

They both looked at him. He shook his head.

"I don't think - " he began.

"We are caretakers, Aonghas," said Dorian severely. "We do not get holidays. If you wanted to drink, Glasgow has pubs. It is not meant to be in our nature to desire *a break*. Even so, we were here. Why did you not tell us?"

"Because I am fed up with this!" cried Aonghas, turning to Leah. "Look at what your world, your city, has turned me into! A... A *bum*."

"A Glaswegian," said Leah. "There's strength in that, and insulting your city does not make you a sound Guardian. If this is something you hate so much, have you ever considered that it was the lack of your protection that helped cause it?"

Aonghas stared at Leah, utterly speechless. The truth of this shone brightly in his mind.

Leah was also startled that she had come to the defence of the city. Maybe it was growing on her.

"Perhaps it is time to take up the mantle again," said Dorian. "Take this poor young man under your wing, so to speak. It is time. It is too late for many, but there is time enough for those still to come."

Aonghas nodded, and his mouth tightened against the first tears to visit him in centuries.

***

Outside, Tearlach caught up with Dylan.

"Fuck aff," said Dylan, walking swiftly into the wind and needling rain. Tearlach put a hand on his arm and spun him around with surprising ease and grace.

"*Dylan Stuart*," said Tearlach. "and you are an honour to the name - but will you not listen to me?"

"Why?" he asked. "What on earth could an 18th-century Highlander possibly have t'say tae me? You dinna ken what heroin is! Ye dinna ken Glesga! Hell, you dinna e'en ken what Irn-Bru is! What can you possibly hae t'say tae me, *Tearlach of Glengoyne?!*"

Tearlach stared at him, in the dark and forbidding Glasgow greylight. The rain was coming down swiftly now, obscuring the black-accented brown buildings, marks of the days when coal was king, and the city suffocated with it.

"When I was a wee boy," said Tearlach, "my clan was attacked in the night. Everyone was slaughtered - my parents, my brothers and sisters. I escaped, over the mountains, to the only other clan who could take me in - the Stuarts. *I escaped alone.* I am alone, Dylan Stuart, like you. My name is Tearlach of Glengoyne, who follows Iain. You are a Stuart. Your people saved me."

Dylan stared at his friend for a moment, at a loss for words.

Then his great seraph wings unfolded to surround them both, shielding them from the rain and the sky.

Dylan smiled, and Tearlach, in the shade of his wings, grinned back at him.

***

The door to the station opened. Leah, Dorian, and Aonghas turned to see Dylan enter with Tearlach. The young man's wings unfolded and shook water everywhere.

"Pardon me," said Dorian. "The carpets were cleaned just this morning."

Leah shot him a look.

"What?" he asked.

"I will work wi' you," Dylan said. "But you'll agree t'dae yir job, an' t' be responsible, Aonghas."

Aonghas stood up.

"I cannot stand for this," he said. "This - young upstart."

"Tak' it or leave it, old man," Dylan replied.

Aonghas crossed his arms.

"I think he's right, Aonghas," said Leah. "You've let the city down."

"Dylan is the hero Glasgow needs," said Dorian, smiling. "Aonghas is the hero Glasgow deserves."

Leah rotated towards him.

"Did you just make a Batman reference?" she asked.

Dorian sniffed.

"I am not entirely devoid of culture, Miss Bishop," he said.

Dylan paced the floor.

"Awright, big man," said Dylan, crossing his arms. "Anyway how come *you* can be drunk an never accidentally summon a *teuchter* fae the past, or anythin'?"

"Practice, my boy," said Aonghas. "Practice."

"Does the package come wi' anythin' besides giant wings?" asked Dylan.

"Yes," said Aonghas. "The first thing you will need is your pouch - used to carry bread and water, sometimes ale or mead. Nowadays I can't get anything out of it besides curry and Buckfast."

"What, you mean this?" asked Dylan. He lifted Aonghas's satchel.

He reached in and pulled out a full lamb and mash meal, never breaking Aonghas's gaze. He handed the food to Tearlach, who began eating it with evident enjoyment.

Aonghas stared at the satchel, then back at Dylan.

"Clearly you need t' stop drinkin' yirsel," said Dylan. "Practice or no'."

He turned to the room at large.

"I'm Glesga's guardian angel the noo," he stated. "Anyone or anythin' tha' stands against Glesga will hafta answer tae me."

***

Dylan looked confident, as if he had found a purpose. The new wings dwarfed him, but somehow he looked *right*. Tearlach stood and went to him.

"This is a great honour, Dylan," said Tearlach gently. "There are very few who can claim it."

Dylan's wings gave a tentative beat.

"Aye?" he said. "It was inevitable, wasn't it?"

"Not if the Guardian hadn't died," said Aonghas. "Sebastian is indeed more powerful than we thought. This was his warning to me. It is on my head, Dylan, both the death of the Guardian and your new responsibility. It is a heavy burden and I would not have wished it upon you."

Dylan took a deep breath, and looked at Tearlach. His eyes sparkled.

"Well," he said. "There's nae use greetin' about what coulda been, or what shoulda been. I reckon you'll tell me what I need tae learn."

Aonghas lifted his head. His elven features cleared, almost into a smile.

"There is nothing either of you can do now about the death of the Guardian," said Tearlach. "The Fae are powerful. In my time, they were still respected and feared. If it is your duty to be eternal guardians of this city, it would be best to work together."

Dylan and Aonghas nodded.

"Shall we?" asked Aonghas.

"Are we free tae go?" asked Dylan.

"I believe so," said Tearlach. He bowed to Magnus.

"Excuse me, my lord," he said, bowing deeply. "May we go?"

Magnus smiled a brilliant smile.

"Oh yes, of course," he said. "My apologies. I wish you luck, Tearlach."

He looked over at Aonghas and Dylan.

"And I am sure I will be seeing the two of you again," he said, with a knowing grin.

"All right, that's our cue," said Aonghas. "Let's go."

The three men left Caledonia Interpol, not quite friends, but not quite enemies either.

***

Dylan's favourite pub was crowded. He had thought it would be fitting to take his friend out for a drink at the same place they had met. He wasn't sure whether becoming Fae, or realising he was Fae, was worthy of celebration, but he felt some kind of drinking session was in order.

Tearlach smiled at Dylan. He raised his beer.

"To you, my friend," Tearlach said, and took a deep draught. He then stared at the glass with extreme distrust.

"Wit's wrang?" asked Dylan through a mouthful of foam.

"What is this?" demanded Tearlach.

"It's beer," Dylan said.

Tearlach stared at his friend as though he was playing a dangerous and not particularly funny practical joke.

"I don't know who's been telling you that, son," said Tearlach, "but this isn't beer."

"Wit d'you mean?"

"Is there a way you can reach back into the past and bring something forward?" asked Tearlach.

"I dinnae ken. I could try."

"See if you can imagine my village, and bring some real beer into this day and age," Tearlach said.

Dylan concentrated, imagining a pristine Highland village and a glassy loch, the sun shining down on green hills and mountains, and then, nestled in the town, the sort of alehouse he'd once seen at a Renaissance festival.

There was a loud pop, and an explosive rustle of feathers. Two tall mugs of foaming beer sat in front of the men, but unfortunately the effort had caused Dylan's wings to appear and knock over a few of their fellow patrons. Tearlach and Dylan looked around, terrified at what might transpire due to this foolish display of power. There was no telling how Glaswegians might react to a ned angel.

The entire pub erupted in applause, even the people who had been knocked down. They touched the long flight feathers of the wings and complimented them on such amazing costumes, what with Dylan's ned angel outfit and Tearlach looking as if he had dressed as the cover of a romance novel for an early Hallowe'en.

Dylan breathed a sigh of relief, and proudly waved his wings a bit. He strangely disliked the lack of them. They felt a part of him and a symbol of what he hoped to become. He had always wanted to do something with his life, to be important somehow. Now, he felt responsible for an entire city, a lynchpin holding it together and helping to improve conditions. He knew the work would be slow and arduous, but he also felt the responsibility, as if he had been born into it - and in a way, he had.

"You'll get stuck like that," said another voice.

Dylan started, and turned to see Aonghas seated at the table. Tearlach pretended there was something very interesting on the ceiling.

"Aonghas! I'm sorry, we were jist-"

"Manifesting your wings for the punters? Trying to order beer from the eighteenth century? Yeah, I got that," said Aonghas. "While you can indeed do that, that's not what you've done."

"Oh?"

"You've created it yourself."

"Wit?"

"You created this beer. You imagined what Scotland was like back then, and you made beer out of it."

Tearlach and Dylan stared at the beer. It did not do anything particularly startling.

"So... this is distilled imaginary Scotland?" asked Dylan.

"Pretty much," said Aonghas, putting a hand to one well-defined cheekbone and leaning against it, amused.

"That's not the important question here," said Tearlach decisively. "The important question is: does it taste any good?"

They looked at the beer again. Aonghas rolled his eyes.

"Wull," said Dylan, rubbing his hands in anticipation. "It looks like it's ma responsibility tae find out. Widnae want the two o' you t' get poisoned, or anythin'."

He lifted the mug to his lips, and took a hesitant swallow.

Then he swiftly downed the entire thing in one go. Dylan had never tasted anything so wonderful in his entire life. Aonghas shook his head, and raised his eyes toward the ceiling.

"A ned angel that can make his own beer," he said. "Glasgow is fortunate."

Chapter Eleven

For Leah, going anywhere with Dorian was an exercise in patience. Men and women would turn to look, wanting to talk to him or touch him, as if he were famous. God forbid he ever take it into his head to wear a kilt. He dealt with all this attention surprisingly well. The age or gender of his admirers did not seem to matter and he managed to dissuade them all with a grace Leah had only read about.

The same could not be said of Magnus.

"Thank you very much," Dorian was saying as yet another woman complimented his choice of jacket. This was strange, given that Victorian outerwear in Glasgow was not so much an appreciated fashion choice as a reason to glass someone in the face. However, people just seemed to like Dorian.

"How you ever catch any criminals or chase them down, I have no idea," Leah muttered, as they slowly cleaved through a crowd of admiring women.

"Chase?" he asked mildly. "Why should I need to chase anyone?"

And suddenly the reason Chief Ben had hired this quiet, non-violent young man was very clear. Employing the selk would be a perfect way to ensure that no criminal ever escaped again.

People would *want* to be caught.

***

Desdemona stepped outside into the mist as it coiled around her like a lover.

She smoked, her green eyes reflecting the orange-red of the burning cigarette. Tendrils of fog curled around the city, a monster waiting silently to consume and obliterate everything familiar.

Dorian approached her at the door to the club, standing in the shadows.

"Yes, what is it now?" she sighed when she recognised Dorian and Leah.

Magnus pushed forward. Desdemona nearly dropped her cigarette.

"Hello," he said. "Ignore my brother. I think we can talk together."

She gave him a once-over, smiled, and walked inside.

She sat down on one of the red sofas away from the bar, where it was quieter. The shisha smoke rose gently from her pipe, the coals in the hookah sizzling softly. She stared at Magnus, drawing her breath in and slowly breathing out, obscuring her bright green eyes.

He smiled at her; lazy, confident. She smiled back.

Desdemona outranked Magnus by a long way, and was far older. Still, it amused her to watch one of the seal-boys try their charms on a *baobhan sith*. He clearly had become far too accustomed to the surrender of mortal women. It had been such a long time since she'd seen him, perhaps he had forgotten her after all these years.

"Oh, let's not talk about the case just yet," he said. "I'd like to know about you. Tell me about yourself. How have you been, Desdemona?"

Desdemona grinned and stayed silent. She wished she had fangs, but she wasn't that kind of vampire.

Magnus cleared his throat.

"So," he said, "let's talk about the case, then."

"I am at your service," she said.

***

Desdemona curled a white hand around a crystal glass, and drank absinthe mixed with blood.

"What more is there to say?" she asked. "Aonghas told you that Sebastian was behind the killings. Sebastian is behind everything. *Everything*. It stands to reason. I don't even know how this is considered a case. It doesn't take a lot of thought."

"Why would Sebastian do something like this? Serial killing?" Magnus asked. "He's more the corporate crime type, fancies himself some kind of Robin Hood."

"If you mean stealing from the rich to give to himself, then maybe," laughed Desdemona. "Now, I don't know why Sebastian would do something like this. I do know that perhaps you ought to be investigating your brother. Now, *that's* criminal."

She exhaled a plume of smoke, staring at Dorian where he stood with Leah near a potted plant. He looked bored and somewhat uncomfortable, while Leah seemed enchanted by the place.

"Dorian?" asked Magnus, looking over his shoulder. "Why is that?"

Desdemona smiled.

"You should know," she said. "If Dorian hasn't told you yet, he really ought to. The world is a big place now and we aren't necessarily the strongest anymore, are we?"

Magnus stared at her, puzzled into silence.

"Well, this has been fascinating," said Desdemona, "but I perform in twenty minutes. See you around, Magnus Grey."

She stood up, set her blood absinthe on the table, and left Magnus alone on the couch. He returned to where Dorian and Leah were standing, leaping over the back of the sofa and grinning at them, a swizzle stick between his teeth.

"She says that it is definitely Sebastian," Magnus said. "He's been here, and she says it's bigger than we think. She also said that I should be investigating you, Dorian. What does she mean?"

Dorian stared at his brother. The silence stretched between them. Leah had to break in.

"What does Dorian have to do with Sebastian?" she asked.

Dorian didn't answer. He turned and left the club without a

word. Magnus seemed to regret his actions and he went after his brother, looking ashamed of himself.

"Where are you going?" Leah called after the two of them, but a reply never came.

***

Leah walked home alone. The rain continued to pour into the night, giving a Monet aspect to the evening. People passed by hurriedly, seeking warmth and shelter. Glasgow on some nights could be warm and beautiful, its cobblestones bathed in orange light, shining in the mist and rain. The shops along Great Western Road were awash in the sunset brilliance of a Glasgow evening, and the patrons of the pubs spilled out into the night, banter interspersed with laughter and the click and flick of lighters in exchange for a story and a quick smoke. The spires of the cathedrals and the red sandstone buildings offered a sense of both history and home. The forests of Kelvingrove Park and the fountains of greenery touching the river as it wound its merry way through the city were all cast in the warmth of a Glasgow twilight, firelit orange, cool in the damp mist of a summer's evening.

Leah opened the door to her room, and shook the water from her umbrella. A chill had set in again, and she went to the counter to make tea. The availability of tea on a cool evening, provided by the hotel, warmed her. Although she was alone, it made her feel less lonely.

***

When the sun began to rise the following morning, Aonghas walked across the long green lawn as the previous night's shadows receded. He stepped inside the People's Palace, where Dylan was waiting for him. Tearlach was beside himself with excitement and joy, like a child at the zoo.

Aonghas handed Dylan the soda he'd purchased from the

corner shop, and passed an orange juice to Tearlach.

"Bloody *hell,*" said Tearlach, impressed. "*Oranges.* What a miraculous time!"

Dylan's wings suddenly appeared with a sound like a feather pillow hitting a wall.

"Gaaaahhh!" he shouted in frustration, nearly tipping over. "I cannae control them!"

"It'll take some time," said Aonghas, drinking from his own bottle. "Though I'm not sure why you chose to have them so large."

"Wull, I didnae ken, did I?" said Dylan. "You said I was a faerie, an' then I kent I read su'n aince about how faeries were really angels or su'n an' I thought *interesting, angels an' faeries* an' there you go."

"Where on *earth* would someone like you read about *that*?" asked Aonghas.

Dylan's wings quivered in annoyance.

"*Someone like me,*" he muttered. "I'll hae you ken I went tae uni. Graduated wi' honours, too, an' I'm only 21."

"Hmm," said Aonghas. "You are certainly surprising."

"Wull, yir no' like any ned I ken either, so we're in guid company," Dylan said. "So - the wings. Is there any way I can change 'em back? Undo it?"

"Unfortunately not," said Aonghas. "They'll look like that until the public perception of angels changes. Angels, unfortunately, are extremely popular so you'll be stuck like that until people decide angels don't have gigantic wings."

"Is tha' how you got yir wings?" asked Dylan. "Because people believe that's wit faeries look like?"

"Yes," he said. "They used to look different, and before that, I had no wings. Fortunately it hasn't had an effect on our size, only the superficial things: clothes, wings, what kind of food we can retrieve from our satchels, although you seem to have challenged that notion. Anyway, one night I was dreaming of home - and I woke up with them."

"Hame?" asked Dylan. "Wit d'you mean? Isnae Glasgow yir

hame?"

Aonghas smiled thinly.

"For centuries, yes," he said. "But my home - and yours - is far away. I mean the land of Faerie. I had dreamed I was there, walking among the soft grasses, and that I was beautiful again. And I woke with dragonfly wings."

"Wull, thanks for the warnin'," Dylan retorted. "I'd'a liked a moment tae think about it!"

Aonghas shrugged.

"It shows the soul of you," he said. "Generally the manifestations are apt. You are a Guardian. It makes sense that you'd take the appearance of an angel."

"Does that mean I hafta wear robes and grow my hair out an'-?" asked Dylan.

"Not unless you want to," said Aonghas.

They walked through the Winter Gardens inside the People's Palace. Tropical plants from around the world towered above them, as the light from a colder sun made prisms through the glass. Glasgow Green was once the province of kings, and the Winter Gardens were a breathtaking example of that history.

Tearlach walked the pathways in wonder. He had never seen anything like most of the plants on display. To him, they seemed from another world, intoxicating and magical. Faeries were a part of his everyday reality, commonplace, and sewn into the fabric of his being. Tropical foliage, however, was as magical and otherworldly to him as the Fae were to the modern world.

"Do you mean to tell me," he said reverently, "that there are people who do not feel the winter's chill? What do they do? How can they drink tea? Perhaps they drink something cooler."

Musing to himself, he wandered off into the labyrinthine display, and Dylan smiled after him.

"Are you gonna come wi' me, t'bring Tearlach home?" Dylan asked Aonghas.

"I might, if I feel like it," replied Aonghas.

"The thing is... I dinnae really want Tearlach t'gae hame," said

Dylan, watching his enthusiastic new friend.

"Tearlach's existence here is causing strange rifts in time, can't you sense it? It feels like swimming upstream."

Dylan considered this. He did detect something wrong around Tearlach, as if he were a pebble causing constant ripples in the air.

"Am I immortal the noo?" he asked, suddenly.

"Yes. And forever young," said Aonghas. "Believe me, it's not what it's cracked up to be."

"Boredom?" asked Dylan.

Aonghas nodded.

"Better than death," said Dylan decisively.

Aonghas shrugged. He wouldn't know.

"There are six Guardians of Glasgow," said Aonghas. "They are served by bodyguards, called the Attendants. If we had a leader, it would be the Gatekeeper - the angel statue in the Gorbals, whose Attendants flank the creature on either side along the buildings."

"Servants?" asked Dylan, looking disgusted. "Nae thanks."

"Dylan, it's always been this way," said Aonghas.

"Tha's nae reason it needs t'stay tha' way," Dylan replied. "I'm not putting anyone, or *anything*, in danger. Nae. I'll do it alane."

Aonghas sighed. *Young people.*

"I don't know how you got here," he said. "I don't know how you ended up a ned, but you are definitely the biggest surprise I've had in all my years of living."

"Or maybe you jist dinnae understand neds," said Dylan. "Everyone thinks terrible things about us, an' sometimes they're right. But we're jist people, like any other people. Being born rich disnae mean being born smart."

"And here's the evidence, in the flesh," said Aonghas. "I wasn't sure at first, but I think I would be proud to work by your side."

"An' I'll be holding you accountable," said Dylan. "Protecting Glasgow is our job."

Aonghas grinned.

"Definitely an angel," he said.

"Are angels real, by the way?" asked Dylan, "I widnae want t' gie offense."

Aonghas just shrugged, as if he knew the answer but wasn't planning to share.

***

Leah found Dorian standing on the Great Western Bridge overlooking the River Kelvin. He seemed different in this light, as though he truly did not belong in this world. Her gaze almost slid off him. He was definitely made of something not human and in the bright, harsh, and silver Scottish light this was very obvious. His skin looked as if it were made of marble.

He was looking into the water of the river as though it were a window to the past.

Leah sat down beside him and waited. She was afraid to say anything. If he wanted to talk, he would.

"Your young man," he said softly, so low she could barely hear him. "Do you still love him after what he's done to you?"

This surprised her. She was expecting a confession, or some explanation of his behaviour with Magnus. She had also not thought much about this, focused as she had always been on the heartbreak and jealousy. When she thought of Adam, it was with pain. She hadn't considered whether that meant she still loved him.

"I suppose I do," Leah said. "But I don't think I could ever be with him again."

Dorian put a white hand on the rail of the bridge. The green foliage surrounded them and creeping plants held the structure in an embrace that could become a chokehold. There were few parts of the city that reminded him of the Fae homeland, but this was one of them. He watched the water coursing beneath him, clear and white, smoothing the rocks below. He sighed, and smiled.

"It has been over one hundred years," said Dorian. "I still remember her. The way she tucked her hair behind her ear, how her eyes lit up when she laughed, the scent of her lily of the valley perfume. Women are not what they were."

He looked at Leah, who remained silent.

"Or perhaps they are what they always have been," said Dorian. "Perhaps new eras do not invent new ways of behaving, just new names for it."

He was silent again for a while, as the Kelvin passed beneath them. Leah wondered if he longed for the sea, if leaving human form to return to the ocean was the selkie way of leaving the world in general. It must be strange, and difficult, to belong to not one world, but two. Perhaps the rivers of Glasgow were the closest he could get to the sea, as it cried out to the wild tide in his veins, the endless deep pull of the water calling him home.

"You said she died of old age," Leah prompted him. She was, after all, a detective.

Dorian stirred, and nodded.

"Yes," he said. "The loss was terrible. A selkie loves just as he did when he was first Taken, hundreds of years later. At least for me, the loss was a natural one, difficult as it was."

"But?" Leah prompted.

Dorian sighed. He turned to his partner.

"Several years ago," he said, "someone began killing the women and men whom the selk belonged to. It was efficient, cold, brutal. Someone was systematically taking the one thing that any of us cared about or lived for. Imagine what it would be like to discover that your young man had been slaughtered - mutilated."

Leah was taken aback. Dorian's dour expression, the rarity of his smile, all led her to surmise that he must have suffered much, but this was more than she had expected. The kind of secret that cut too deep. She wondered what else he had seen, over his long life.

She thought about what he had said for a moment, and shuddered. Losing Adam had been difficult. She looked forward to the day when she would wake up and not feel the dagger of loss in her stomach. Still, he lived and he was safe. To have lost him in the way Dorian described... even with the heartbreak, it was too horrible to contemplate.

"The selk, as species, feel like you do, but with ten times the intensity," Dorian said. "No one loves like we do. And in these particular cases, they were relationships in which the selkies were in bliss, for their humans loved them in return. They were perfect loves."

"Why would someone murder them?" Leah asked.

"I don't know. We never found out. But the selk involved were... broken by the experience, forever. Now, they seem... out of place, misaligned, as if they don't belong. *Old*."

Leah stared at Dorian.

"Magnus."

Dorian nodded.

"I admit, I lied when I said he was Untaken," he said. He studied the water below, and Leah watched him. She often found patience could encourage more of a story she wanted to hear.

"He loved Hazel deeply," sighed Dorian. "She was the first to be killed. I never told him how she died. When the murders stopped, I thought that was the end of it."

"Why wouldn't you do something about it yourselves? Because the selk are too peaceful?" Leah asked.

"No," said Dorian. "Because we are too dangerous."

"Dangerous?" Leah asked, incredulous, looking at his beautiful tailcoat and shining pocketwatch.

"I realize how we may seem to you," said Dorian. "A selkie at rest is peaceful and loving. If you take something from us, especially our lovers, we become deadly, more violent than a terrible storm. Rage as endless and deep as the sea. Together, united as one, we could be the downfall of mankind."

Leah shook her head, trying to imagine an army of the selk, dressed in clothes from a variety of time periods, somehow destroying the world. It was impossible.

"Okay, so... say I believe you," she told him. "Who would do something like that?"

"We believe now that it was Sebastian," said Dorian coldly.

"Magnus doesn't know that Hazel's death was only the first in a pattern. We kept it secret from the world at large because, well, some of the selk would not sit by quietly."

"Well, maybe you shouldn't have," Leah said. "Sebastian is at it again."

Dorian turned to her.

"Many years ago," said Dorian, "when Magnus and I were just pups, we swam in the shallows of Seal-Hame. Magnus always helped me when I wasn't quick enough to catch a fish, or when there were humans nearby.

'One day, we were basking on the beach near Kintyre. It was a long white stretch of sand. There are many places there to bask and sun ourselves, large rocks scattered across the beach. I remember the day. The sea was so blue, and the islands in the distance grey on the water. We were sunning ourselves when a human crept up behind us with a rock, intending to take my pelt, which we shy away from at the best of times. If a human steals our pelts, they can enslave us."

Leah nodded. She knew the lore.

"He would have dashed my brains out. He was a seal-hunter. The hunter did not know we were selk, although this was a strange thing, since during those times, most humans considered it a dangerous business to kill the seals, fearful of provoking the wrath of the Fae. There are those of us who are not selk, of course... or so I have been told. Thus far, every grey seal I have met has turned out to be a selkie.

'I did not sense the man approaching. My skills were not as honed then as they are now, and Magnus had spent far more time among the humans than I had. He came out of his skin so quickly I could hear the rending of it. It must have caused him considerable pain. Roaring, he appeared as if by magic, a tall and beautiful young man with the rage and fear of his brother's murder in his great dark eyes."

Dorian gestured idly at the water with a bare hand, and a tiny whirlpool formed beneath it.

"The man fell to his knees, begging forgiveness," said Dorian.

"For some reason, my brother stayed his hand. The man took to his heels, ran away, and, I am sure, never tried to hurt another seal again."

Dorian stared into the water, beyond his reflection there.

There was a strange, low, keening sound.

Leah looked over her shoulder, at the people walking past, at the trees, and then slowly realised the sound was coming from Dorian. Sure enough, the keening noise came again. It was unearthly, unsettling, and heartbreaking to hear.

"Dorian," she said. "What are you doing?"

"Singing," he replied. "Haven't you ever heard seals sing?"

Leah thought back to the few times she had been on the coast and could not remember.

"Seals sing rarely," he said. "To tell each other stories, or for great love, to coo at your lover, or for great loss."

The strange keening came again, building in that inhuman voice, an ethereal song of grief and loss that brought Leah near tears, though she did not understand a word of it.

Chapter Twelve

onghas walked with Dylan and Tearlach as they talked about the world and how it had changed since Tearlach's time. They left the People's Palace laughing together. It began to rain, soft at first, kissing the skin, until the wind picked up and the sky darkened. As the sky opened, Dylan's wings appeared with the sound of rushing wind, and he sheltered Tearlach beneath them.

"Let's get ice cream, what d'you think?" said Dylan.

"In this weather?" asked Aonghas. Dylan laughed.

"Mate, any weather's guid weather for ice cream," he said. "Wit d'ye think, Tearlach?"

"That sounds wonderful," said Tearlach, "What is it?"

Dylan grinned.

"You'll see!" he said. "There are so many more flavours than when I was a bairn, you cannae imagine the difference since then..."

Aonghas walked behind them, silent. The Trooping Faerie sighed. He knew what he had to do, and that Dylan wouldn't like it. He touched the other man on the shoulder.

"Dylan," he said. "We need to talk."

Dylan gave him an aggrieved look, but they stopped on the street, Tearlach reluctantly turning out from under the canopy of Dylan's wings. Aonghas nodded to the Highlander, who went to look at the window display of a charity shop with all the interest of someone who had never seen modern clothing before.

"Wit d'you want noo?" Dylan asked. "Yir ruinin' the moment."

"He can't stay, Dylan," said Aonghas. "He's not meant to be here."

Dylan stared at Aonghas in defiance, but the older man held his gaze. Dylan wilted, his wings slumping. He rubbed his face and nodded.

"Aye," Dylan sighed. "I can feel it, too. Wit d'you want me t'dae about it?"

"You need to open a rift in time. You're powerful enough. I'll have to help you, but Tearlach needs to go home."

Dylan gazed at his new friend, currently occupied with staring bemusedly at a PVC corset. Dylan's eyes went soft and fond.

The angel turned to Aonghas in rebellion.

"Nae!" he said. "I wi'nae. I can tak' care o' him. If I sen' him back he'll be killed in some war, an' he's only jist twenty."

"I know," said Aonghas. "I know it's difficult, but it's not right to keep him here. He doesn't belong."

Dylan looked at Tearlach again, and his heart warmed as he watched the man who was obviously a warrior in his own time, filled with childlike wonder in this strange new world.

Dylan's mouth set. Tearlach should be a hero, in a time and place that would honour his name. Here among the disused beer cans and twisted metal broken alleyways of what Dylan could offer him, a life easily forgotten, living off the £5 specials and sometimes splashing out on the weekends for the fancy £10 gourmet M&S meals with a bottle of wine... Dylan halted this line of thought before it depressed the hell out of him.

He had nothing to offer Tearlach but the shelter of his wings.

"I suppose yir right," sighed Dylan, resigned. "How?"

Aonghas motioned with his head, and Dylan followed.

He watched as Aonghas lifted a hand, and *turned the earth*, Glasgow fading out and green hills fading in, green foliage and the bright blue of a summertime loch emerging from the city, as though Aonghas had turned the handle of a door. The Trooping Faerie looked at him, and suddenly Dylan could see Aonghas as he truly was: the power radiating from him, the warmth and the heat, intense beauty alight within him, staring out through foreign eyes.

Dylan winced, and looked away.

❀ CHAPTER TWELVE ❀

"Now, Dylan!" said Aonghas. "Before it's too late!"

Dylan grabbed Tearlach by the arm and his friend, startled, followed him. Aonghas stepped forward with them, and the world turned inside out.

A moment later, they were all standing next to an enormous tree in the midst of a field dotted with sheep. The sun was shining gloriously on gently rolling hills, and reflected in the ripples of the loch below. The land was hemmed in by mountains and ringed with white clouds. It was midsummer, and the freshness of the air, the scent of broom and heather, made Dylan's eyes water. Aonghas smiled. This was a time in which he had been both loved and feared.

Tearlach stared around himself in wonder. He seemed to breathe everything in, the flowers and the grass. He turned around slowly, taking in the bright green forest and hills, the blue of the sky, the quiet sounds of the earth. His eyes went wide.

"I'm home! Well done, Dylan!" he cried, and then broke into a grin. "And there's my cow!" He turned to look at his friend. His expression softened.

"You're welcome to stay," he said, a little hesitant. "You would make a fine warrior, and my hearth will always have a place for you beside it."

Dylan looked at Aonghas, who shook his head.

"Believe me," said the Trooping Faerie. "I would stay myself, if I could. Those ripples you sensed in the future are nothing compared to what you would do if you remained in the past. Say your goodbyes. I will be on the lookout. You don't have much time."

And with that, Aonghas left them to say farewell in private.

Tearlach sighed.

"It seems we were fated to meet this just once," he said. "That is sometimes the way of magic. I will not forget you, Dylan Stuart."

Dylan stared up at the baby blue sky, into the cool white sunlight of the Highlands.

113

"I wi' nae greet," murmured Dylan, almost to himself. "I wi' nae."

He made a snuffling noise, and Tearlach suddenly threw himself into his friend's arms.

"Thank you for everything, Dylan," said Tearlach. "You are a true friend."

After a moment, he returned the embrace, his eyes shut against the treacherous tears he knew would come.

"You remember tae write," Dylan said. He reluctantly let go.

"I will learn how just for you," said Tearlach, holding him at arm's length. "Please feel free to visit anytime. What stories I'll have to tell!"

He began to walk away across the beautiful glen.

"They wi'nae believe you," said Dylan, shaking his head.

At this, Tearlach turned around. Dylan looked at him, a Highland warrior framed in the strength of the mountains, with the grass and the loch rolling out behind him, the sun making a halo of his long, flowing hair. Tearlach grinned at his friend.

"Oh, I don't know," he said. "People in my time still believe in faeries."

He raised a hand in farewell, and Dylan smiled, the tears flowing now. He raised his own hand in reply, and watched his new friend walk out of his life and into history.

Aonghas ran up to Dylan, out of breath.

"Dylan, we need to go," he said. "There isn't much time."

Dylan sighed, and watched Tearlach walk off across the field, green and shining in the late afternoon sun. He sniffed loudly. Putting his hand inside the pocket of his hoodie, he touched something cold. He withdrew the can of Irn-Bru he had taken from Tearlach and solemnly cracked it open.

"Farewell thee, noble soul," he said, toasting his friend as he took a sip. "The best man I have ever known."

He poured out the remainder of the can, soaking the green earth, and then knelt down and set it at the base of the tree.

He nodded at Aonghas.

"Right," he said. "Glesga's waitin'."

They walked forward together. The world turned inside-out, and they were standing in the street again.

Dylan took a deep breath, and looked around at the modern city. He shook his head at how sudden endings could be.

Aonghas turned to Dylan, and awkwardly tried to put a comforting arm around his shoulder.

"I'm awright. I'm awright!" cried Dylan, pushing him away. "Get aff us, ye great faerie."

Chapter Thirteen

The call had come in late that evening. Another corpse. It had been a miserable business, the neighbours alerting them to the fact that the door to 2A hadn't opened in a few weeks, and that there was a disturbing smell coming from the flat. They had had to break in and the door had to be pushed open past all the mail that had piled up on the floor. While forcing open the door, they had seen a pair of legs on the tiles, halfway out of the bathroom. It seemed that this one had been there a long time.

"Another Fae," murmured Dorian. "How is Sebastian doing this? It's like they just lay down and die."

"No blood, no struggle," agreed Leah. "There are no markings of any kind."

"What do you think, Chief?" asked Dorian, looking up.

"If Aonghas is right, and Sebastian has confessed to these murders," said the chief, "it stands to reason that it's time to talk to Magnus about what happened to Hazel."

"We're only going on a theory, that it was Sebastian back then," said Dorian. "His activities only became clear several years after her death, and we assumed he had something to do with it because of his prominence in the criminal world."

"Yes, but criminals don t become the heads of a crime syndicate overnight," said Leah, "so he could have been active before that."

"Perhaps," said Dorian, "but Aonghas is right. Murder was never part of Sebastian's repertoire. There is often a modicum of violence when a criminal like him becomes powerful, but as far as we are aware, his takeover was far more corporate than bloody. Part of the mystery of Sebastian is how he has been able to influence people, including the Fae, for so long without any kind of violent intervention, as far as we know."

"From what Aonghas says, it sounds to me like it's primarily a large network of favours," said Leah. "It's amazing how heavily some things can weigh on the mind and spirit, even for the Fae. In fact, the Fae might feel it even more keenly, given that their lifespans are so much greater than those of humans. It's still possible that Sebastian had a hand in what happened to the lovers of the Taken selk so long ago."

"Perhaps we were wrong in shielding Magnus from Sebastian, Dorian," Chief Ben said, in a voice that came from the depths of the earth.

Dorian nodded.

"I will explain everything to him," said the selkie. "He is my brother, after all."

The door opened and Magnus stepped inside. Leah could see a strange light around him, his skin giving off a slow golden luminescence, what Dorian had called *moonlight*. She gasped inwardly when she realised this must have been what Tearlach was talking about, *and she could see it too.*

The ethereal golden glow, smudging the barest edges of his face as he moved in poetry. That soft smile, the merriment in his eyes, the edges turned up as they crinkled slightly. God, he was beautiful. Leah would always remember how he looked, framed in the doorway, the moment before Dorian spoke.

Magnus had not moved a muscle as Dorian explained, but Leah saw the glow dim, as though filling with tears. Dorian's corresponding silvery glow was almost nonexistent. Dorian's eyes remained fastened on his brother's.

"We wanted to protect you," Dorian finished. "I am sorry, Magnus. I did what I thought was best, but now..."

Magnus's head sunk slowly to his chest. He was silent for a very long time. He looked up. Leah was shocked by the ice blue colour of his eyes, pale as water, lightning-struck.

"I know, brother," he said. "You are forgiven."

He turned on his heel and left the flat. The three of them stood quietly together, unsure of what to say.

❀ CHAPTER THIRTEEN ❀

The door opened again, as Milo arrived with Geoffrey and the rest of the forensics team.

Geoffrey nodded to Leah and blushed as he passed them. Leah smiled tightly and then returned her attention to the conversation.

"Magnus took that pretty well," she said. Dorian had been speaking in a low whisper to the chief, and she was surprised when she finally caught the words.

"What are we going to do?" he was asking. "We knew this might happen."

"What? Have I missed something again?" Leah asked.

"His eyes. You must have seen them," said Chief Ben.

"Yes?" she said, puzzled.

"His eyes are brown, like all the selk," said Dorian.

"They're blue or grey-"

"No," said Dorian. "They are brown. That ice blue colour is the warning of the gathering storm. It also means that the selk know. All of them, all over the world. We have to find Sebastian before they do. They are coming for him. And they are angry."

"How are we going to find Sebastian?" Leah asked, but Dorian was already out the door.

Leah ran down the stairs and flung the door open, where she nearly ran into the selkie, standing very still on the pavement outside.

Plastered all over the buildings, the lampposts, and the subway entrance, was graffiti that read SEBASTIAN.

"Who did this?" Leah asked. "There was hardly any time! We only went inside twenty minutes ago!"

"Someone must have seen us together at Desdemona's club," he said. "That's the only time we were speaking of him. Someone else could have heard."

"There's no guarantee of that! Desdemona said she didn't know anything," said Leah.

"She's *baobhan sith*, Leah," said Dorian. "She hates me. She has every reason to lie. *Every* reason."

"You are going to have to tell me that story someday," said

Leah.

"Someday," agreed Dorian. "Come on. Sebastian or one of his people might still be at Desdemona's."

"They'll be long gone by now, if they're smart," she said.

"For the sake of the world, let's hope they're not," said Dorian, and he ran up Buchanan Street with Leah close behind him.

**

Dorian and Leah burst into the warm, candlelit darkness of the restaurant. A crowd of unsavoury characters sat in the shadows watching the performance, while the regular customers sat at the good tables. Desdemona's club was a combination of restaurant, hookah bar, and nightclub during the early hours of the morning. It was a place of employment for monsters all over the world of a female or nonbinary appearance, Desdemona herself being an eldritch horror with a vaguely female shape rather than any particular gender. She often began to form into something far more monstrous if you looked out of the corner of your eye, but if you focused on her she looked like she was a woman. Probably.

It was a safe place for those seeking shelter, and they found welcome and understanding there. Since the club was a refuge of sorts for monsters escaping bad situations, it was often the best place in the city for the police to learn information. This information was freely given with the tacit agreement of Interpol to look the other way in regards to the questionably legal goings-on of the club. Richly decorated and warm, it was always filled with smoke and gave visitors the impression they were visiting another world, stepping through a doorway in time to catch a glimpse of magic through the haze. Desdemona stood guard over them all, no stranger to both sides of the law herself.

When Leah and Dorian arrived, the *baobhan sith* was finishing her set to appreciative applause. Another dancer took to the stage as Desdemona noticed the detectives standing in the doorway. She gestured towards the back of the restaurant, and they met her there.

"What are you doing here?" she hissed. "Do you have any idea what kind of danger you're in? What kind of danger you've put *me* in?"

"Shut up or I'll stake you," Leah said. "Sebastian or one of his people was here when we visited. Tell us what's going on or I will introduce you to a crucifix."

Desdemona stared down at this tiny defiant human woman. The vampire sighed and leaned against the wall, crossing her arms.

"Look, I can't tell you much," she said. "He could kill me, too."

"We'll protect you," Leah promised.

Desdemona just laughed, her green eyes blazing bright.

"From Sebastian?" she said. "I think I'll take my chances. News of your rude interruption will reach him quickly. You really ought to be more circumspect, officers."

"You must tell us," said Dorian. "Magnus knows that Sebastian killed Hazel. The selk are on the march."

Desdemona stared at him.

"You're kidding," she said. "Why would Sebastian want to destroy the world? Everyone knows the selk are powerful, and like nuclear weaponry, probably best left undisturbed. The selk will decimate anyone and anything in their path."

"I think that is an unfortunate consequence, rather than Sebastian's motivation," said Dorian. "But the selk will tear the world apart to find him. We need to find him first."

"And then what?" she asked. "The only thing you can do is sacrifice him to the selk. Your people are as ancient as mine and Scottish blood runs strong with the thirst for sacrifice. You know that as well as I do. The selk, harmless lovers. Ha! That's rich. We're the ones who get the bad press. Bite, drink, a human lost here and there. We're solitary hunters and we don't take more than we need. Your people get all the beautiful songs and you're the ones capable of destroying the world."

"My people are not vermin or parasites that feed on the human race," snarled Dorian.

"Oh, and feeding on love? That's not being a parasite?" Desdemona shot back.

"Okay, okay!" Leah cried. "The point is, we need to find him. We'll figure out how to stop the selk somehow."

"Good luck," said Desdemona, rolling her eyes. "All I know is that a guy comes here sometimes, he works for Sebastian, and he buys information from me."

She caught Leah's disdainful gaze.

"Don't look at me like that," she said. "I'm on your side, but I have to survive. He could kill me too, you know."

"What kind of information have you given him?" Leah asked.

"Mainly what the police know," she said. "If you want my opinion, Sebastian will only be found if he wants to be. And I think, luckily for you, he does."

"You mean we're walking into a trap," Leah said.

"No," said Desdemona. "I mean I think he wants to be caught, and he wants *you* to catch him."

Dorian followed Leah out the door. The sun was setting, and Glasgow was aflame in orange and red. The red stones of the buildings glowed in the late afternoon light. The selkie put a hand through his hair, and then shook his head.

"Why not just turn himself in, if he wants to be caught? There's some trick in this," he said. "Desdemona knows more than she is saying, I'm sure of it."

"Yes, but there is nothing much we can do, is there?" Leah replied. "It's our job. Catch the bad guys."

"I don't like it," he said. "But it must be done. Let's get back to Caledonia, and see if we can track Sebastian down. All over the world, the selkies will be coming for him."

Seoul, South Korea

He'd been away from Scotland a long time.

Selkies, like the human Scots, had travelled the world and found a place to thrive in every corner of every nation.

❧ CHAPTER THIRTEEN ❧

It had been centuries since he felt the call.

He had wandered the crowded and carnival markets of Asia for decades, where the turbulent colours, the bright neon, the shouts and scents all combined to lose a man forever, like so many had already been lost. There were so many attractions, so many vices and desires fulfilled, until only the shell of the person remained.

But there was nothing in this wild world for him and no vice ensnared his soul.

Only her. *Always* her.

The thin, sweet-faced young man pushed the glass door of the corner shop open and a bell sounded. He regarded the array of bottles in the cooler and made his choice. As the cashier was ringing up the purchase, she noticed him go very still. He was handsome, she thought, and seemed indescribably dangerous.

He stared through her.

"Sir?" she asked, in Korean. The young man did not reply. He turned and walked out the door.

She saw he had left his change on the counter, and when she ran into the street to return it to him, he had vanished. She never forgot him, or his beauty, and he visited her in dreams for the rest of her life, when she had a bad day and needed comfort, there he was. She never saw him outside of dreams, but loved him from that moment and for the rest of her life.

Island of Santorini, Greece

"We're out of milk," called the dark-haired man, peering into the refrigerator.

"I'll get some at the store," came a male voice in reply, his husband, who was upstairs, looking for a tie.

The man at the refrigerator turned and smiled as his son looked up at him. The little boy's face was smeared with spaghetti sauce and he giggled, displaying tiny white teeth. The proud father could already see it there, the magic in those eyes.

123

The large brown eyes of his son, who he would one day take to the sea, to Scotland, to teach the ways of his *other* family.

There was a crash as the plates fell from his hands and shattered across the kitchen floor. His son looked up into his father's staring eyes, and watched as he walked out of the room, to the front door, opening and then shutting it behind him.

"Are you going to get the milk then?" called his husband, as the tiny selkie in his high chair giggled and threw his spoon into the mess on the kitchen floor.

New York, New York

He was beautiful. Beautiful and always young.

They all were, of course.

Marion had asked, before. Why he still looked so handsome, and young, the same as the day they had met at Coney Island in 1934 and he'd already bought her an ice cream cone. She had smiled, brushing tears from her cheek. Those tears, the tears that had called him. All she knew was that there was a handsome young man in a flatcap offering her a melting ice cream cone and grinning at her in the hot summer sunlight. She thought him overdressed then, she thinks him overdressed now. She says so, when he visits.

They won't let him stay, not overnight. The hospital has rules.

He never told her, but he suspects Marion knows. She was always very clever.

The sigh of the respirator filled the room. She opened her eyes, and there he was, so handsome, like that day on the pier, dark eyes dancing.

She sighed. She knew her face was no longer that of the young girl crying over a foolish lost love, smooth and flawless. Her skin had wrinkled, and her hands felt like cool paper, the skeleton evident beneath them now, the folds of age apparent.

And he looked down and still saw only radiant beauty, only the face of the gorgeous girl he was to belong to forever, that day he brought her ice cream. He smiled, and took her hand.

"How do you feel about chocolate?" he whispered, just as he did on that first day, so many years ago, as he handed her the ice cream cone.

She closed her eyes with a smile.

"I never liked it one bit," she said, just as she did then, and sighed, her hand tightening briefly in his.

He felt the tiny cracks that would break him, as she died.

Today, he would not feel the loss, or the grief, not till those cracks had spread and consumed him, but he was lucky. Many selk did not accomplish *last breath*, that final moment which binds forever, and holds the seal-folk safe from the darkness.

His tears were real and hot, and splashed onto her hand as he held it to his cheek.

Suddenly he stood, his dark eyes bright. He fought it, fought against it for all he was worth, but he could not resist. He reached out for her, though he knew she was no longer there, and he managed to whisper *my love, I am sorry* before the wave of magic swept his independence from beneath his feet.

He walked out into the ward, away from the insistent sound of the machine, and down the white hospital hallway without mentioning to the nurse that Marion was gone.

Scottish Highlands

From the cold depths, in the darkness, they emerged from the sea.

The sand was fine and white beneath the roll of their bellies, and the gory, wet sound of fingers pulling through seal-flesh was punctuated by the waves. Slick-skinned, the young men unfolded from their seal-bodies, and stood white and slender under a cold and cursed moon. The sea was endlessly green beyond the darkness, where death awaited those who ventured too far.

The men turned as one body, a compass-point, and walked together in the darkness. The lonely roads were filled with those eyes, haunted and haunting. Anyone who happened upon them felt the dread of times long past, when the people's hearts beat in fear of meeting the Fair Folk on the roadways. So many years had passed, and yet the terror remained the same, beating in time with human blood. Those pale and hollow faces of indescribable beauty told anyone with sense to step aside, to go back, and to place their grandparents' iron horseshoe above their doors.

The walk was long, and uneventful. The selkie-men found clothes along the way. In this cantrip of pain and grief, every seal answered the call, and the pull of the magic. It guided them onwards in the darkness to the orange sea of light that was Glasgow. They did not tire, nor eat or drink. They had one purpose.

They found him, after days and nights of walking. They found him in the city, just as the sun was going down. The first of the seals began to surround him, a single man who stood beneath the statue of St. George, and they focused their ice-blue eyes on his soul.

***

"Dorian?" asked Leah. His eyes had glassed over, rolling to blue. He did not respond to her, but turned and walked off.

"Dorian!" Leah called out, and followed him. She turned the corner to see Dorian standing with a group of men.

They were all in a small park. A statue of St. George stood in the centre, green from age. Encircled on all sides by these dark men was a thin and cowering figure. Magnus stood closest to him, his face expressionless, his eyes dead blue flames with the souls of the ocean's drowned behind them.

Leah recognised the target instantly, and rushed to intervene.

"Geoffrey!" Leah cried. "Stop! It's Geoffrey, from forensics!"

"Leah? What's going on?!" Geoffrey cried. "I was getting a sandwich at the store and they started surrounding me. Magnus?"

Magnus said nothing. Lightning flashed in the ice of his eyes.

Leah looked at the selk now, so terrible, like their forebears on the islands. She remembered how she had felt when Dorian stood with his brother in the cantrip to recall Scotland's history, and the mild storm they had raised on the Clyde. Now, she could sense, more than hear, the low and tangible threat, the ancient drums of a people who still remembered clan, and home, and human sacrifice.

"There must be some mistake," said Leah. "Magnus, stop this! It's *Geoffrey*."

"It is him," Magnus said in a dead voice. "*Look at him.*"

The beautiful men stood in lock formation, dead gazes fixed on the target. Geoffrey looked terrified.

Leah suddenly realized that she and Geoffrey were the only humans present. They were alone, amidst a race of beings with power they could not comprehend, none of whom would step aside.

Geoffrey's blue eyes looked out at her from behind his glasses, his brown hair messy. He still wore his lab coat and a white button-down shirt. He looked pathetic and very frightened.

"I'll think of something," Leah said to him, and looked around herself at the silent seal-people.

The last rays of the sun had disappeared. Geoffrey was surrounded by the selk, backed against the statue. They were beautiful, white as marble, their long black locks curling around their faces, their eyes the colour of the storm. Leah wondered why they hesitated to strike. More selk were joining the group, walking into the circle from every direction.

Geoffrey's face... *changed*.

"Striking me when I am down, that is inexcusable," he said with a laugh, removing his glasses. "And you are supposed to be such a wonderful and kind race. Let your friend see how terrible you have become."

"Geoffrey?" Leah asked, lamely.

He looked down at her and grinned.

"The human recruit," he said. "Who is Geoffrey, after all?"

"You are," she said, confused. "We work together."

"Ah, yes," he said. "Leah Bishop. My name is Sebastian, perhaps you've heard of me? I believe we'll have to call off our date. You think someone would fancy you? I could never befriend anyone who was in league with these... *things*."

Leah suddenly realised that he was supernatural and he didn't know it.

"Call off your dogs," said Sebastian.

There was a dull pain in Leah's heart but she stepped forward anyway. She'd be damned if she allowed her emotions to get the better of her.

"What for? I thought you wanted them this way," said Leah. "Angry, violent, willing to destroy the world just to hunt you down. The selk are noble. They would do anything for one of their own."

"*Noble?*" he laughed. "I don't know who's been spinning *that* story, but they are far from noble. They are vicious. They are betrayers and thieves. You know something about betrayal, Miss Bishop."

Leah's eyes narrowed. She heard a strange sound and turned to the crowd of seal-men. The eyes of the selk flashed a warning fire, their hard faces a reminder of the deadliness of the Highland Scots in battle. Each mouth was a hard, firm line, beautiful and terrible.

"*Ask them*," said Sebastian, gesturing in disgust at the seal-men. "*Ask them* about what they have done, in the name of *love and loyalty*. You really think a race that causes shipwrecks is noble? And what of the other destruction they have caused? You're alone, Leah. Alone with me. The only humans, the only ones with a conscience."

"*You think you're human?*" Leah hissed. "We're not alike, you and I. And the selk are set to destroy you. It seems like you are the one at a disadvantage."

"Do they seem gentle to you?" asked Sebastian, "Beautiful? I assure you, they are *monsters* just like every other foul thing in their world."

She wondered whether she should let the selk take him, if he wanted to be caught. Magnus and Dorian were gone, as empty as standing stones, as solid as history.

Leah stepped into the ring of seal-folk. They did not turn or look in her direction, focused entirely on Sebastian.

He grinned. Leah suddenly felt uncertain. Something was wrong. A human faced with all the selk in the world after him would not be so confident. Perhaps he *did* know he was supernatural, after all.

"How weak you are," he said, and around him, the selk began to fall.

Leah looked around herself in a panic, as the seal-men clutched at their hearts. She sensed clouds building on the horizon of her mind. Suddenly a tempest of memories washed over her. She was lost, then, on a storm-tossed sea.

Adam took her hand as they walked through the Christmas market together, laughing at some joke she couldn't remember, so warm in the cold.

He handed her tea as she stood at the window.

"Heartbroken," said Sebastian, as the selk went to their knees. Some lay on the ground, gasping for air.

"So easily controlled," he murmured.

He was smiling at her across the table in the candlelight.

They talked about their honeymoon and what they could afford, it didn't matter as long as they were somewhere together...

And the spell broke in Leah suddenly, like sunlight cutting through the cracks in the clouds.

Stark white hands clutched at Sebastian's chest, long talons digging into his skin. Perfect red lips grazed Sebastian's ear. He was dragged backwards, struggling.

"A weakness, I assure you, I do not share," Desdemona snarled into his ear.

She smiled and breathed him in, her talons against him and her mouth at the pulse point on his neck, his veins throbbing with the hard beating of his heart.

Her tongue snaked out and tasted his skin.

The *baobhan sith* felt a hand on her shoulder. Startled, she looked around, and saw Leah Bishop looking up at her, somehow having caught the winds of the storm.

"I'll take it from here," said Leah, gasping for breath, staring out from the tempest within.

Desdemona looked at her as if seeing her for the first time. A smile crossed her features and she nodded at Leah in approval.

"*Human,*" she said, rolling the word around in her mouth as if it meant something new to her.

"You're stronger than I thought. You should have just let me kill him, clean and easy."

"And illegal," said Leah.

"Since when do I care about the law?" Desdemona shrugged.

"Since when did you care about the selk?" Leah shot back.

"Do I?" she asked, an eyebrow arched. "I was passing by. I was hungry, he was convenient. You're welcome."

She pushed him into Leah's hands and walked off down the street, hips ticking in time to music they could not hear, lighting a cigarette as she went.

Sebastian looked down at Leah, but did not struggle or make a move to escape.

Leah unhooked her handcuffs and arrested him. She led him away in silence.

The selk were motionless, staring at the spot where he had been standing. Leah cast a glance over her shoulder, and saw Dorian and Magnus faintly glowing in the evening light.

***

Chief Ben met Leah at the door of the precinct. He gazed for a long time at the body of Geoffrey, with the soul of Sebastian now looking out from behind his eyes.

Leah pushed Sebastian into a cell. He put a hand against the glass and looked mournfully out at her. She turned the lock and walked back to where Chief Ben was waiting.

"Sebastian," grumbled Chief Ben ponderously. "I can't say I am pleased to meet him."

Leah looked at her boss.

"Do you mean you knew Geoffrey was Sebastian?" Leah said. "You don't seem surprised."

"I didn't know before," said the chief. "But it is obvious now. Can't you see the light around him? His aura, for want of a better word."

Leah sat down heavily in a chair. She rested her chin on her hand. She looked over at the glass cell, at Geoffrey or Sebastian. He looked defeated. His eyes were rimmed with red as though they were filling with tears.

"Is there a way to make Geoffrey the primary personality?" Leah asked. "A way to separate them and destroy Sebastian?"

"I'm afraid not, Leah," said Chief Ben. "Any spell will only have the effect of reverting Sebastian to himself. Geoffrey does not exist."

"But Geoffrey doesn't know that?" Leah asked.

"No," said the chief. "It's a pity, really it is."

"So... what is Sebastian?" she asked, "I can tell he's not human."

"He's a new kind of monster," said Chief Ben. "Milo was right. There's no word for him yet. Folklore and stories need emotional impact, solid belief, some kind of trauma, perhaps, to become a reality. He has secrets I'd like to know."

Leah nodded to Chief Ben, weary. With a heavy heart, she left the station for the night.

She stood outside, her breath turning to mist in the morning greylight, the air cool and damp upon her cheek. She needed answers, but at the same time, she needed sleep. She was dead on her feet. She walked back to her hotel as Glasgow stirred in waking.

Upon reaching her room, she collapsed onto her bed. She slept, and for the first time did not dream of Adam, but of creatures beyond human knowledge. It was a nightmare, but better than the alternative.

Chapter Fourteen

he turned around as the cell door opened.

"Hello, Miss Leah," he said. So it was Geoffrey she was speaking to. She wasn't sure if this would make it easier, or more difficult, to do her job.

"Do you understand what's happened, Geoffrey?" she asked.

"No, Miss Leah," he said. "I woke up here in the cell. Did I drink too much last night?"

Leah looked into blue eyes so honest and trusting that she began to lose faith in what she had seen the night before. She sighed and pulled up a chair in front of him, indicating that he should also sit down. Geoffrey sat. The earnest expression in his eyes was heartbreaking.

"Geoffrey," she said softly. "It's you."

He held her gaze, uncomprehending. Leah tried again.

"You're Sebastian. You're the serial killer," she said.

Geoffrey started, thunderstruck. His face drained of colour.

"But no," he said. "I'm Geoffrey. Geoffrey Worthington, from Basingstoke."

"I know you think that," said Leah. "I know it seems real, but Geoffrey, you're Sebastian."

"But I have memories of my childhood!" he cried, railing against the truth of it. "The garden, my mum, the first girl I ever - I ever - "

He paused, looking at Leah, and blushed crimson.

"How do you know?" he asked.

"Because I arrested you," she said. "Because you have magic, and you nearly killed us all."

Geoffrey blanched at this, horrified.

"I would never," he whispered.

"Maybe you wouldn't," said Leah, "but Sebastian would.

You're dangerous."

There was fear in Geoffrey's eyes.

"I wish it were different," said Leah. "Believe me, I do. Maybe because-"

"Maybe because I'm a fiction?" Geoffrey said, "Which one of us is real? Geoffrey or Sebastian? I *feel* real."

Leah clenched her teeth.

"Sebastian," she said. "I'm sorry, Geoffrey. You're a part of him, you just don't remember."

Geoffrey stared at her for a moment.

"Magic?" he asked simply, and she nodded.

He looked up at her, misery in those brilliant blue eyes.

"Well," he said. "Good job team! We caught him."

Leah couldn't look at him. Geoffrey was a genuinely good person, with a good heart. He was a man she could have trusted. She wondered what must have happened to Sebastian, if Geoffrey was a part of him, and what kind of desperation had turned him evil enough to splinter his personality.

"Miss Leah, I am dreadfully sorry," he said. "I think I will have to cancel our date."

Leah smiled despite herself, and nodded.

"It's all right, Geoffrey," said Leah, and she hoped it sounded more reassuring than it felt.

It didn't seem like enough.

"You know I have to-" she said.

Geoffrey's expression lost its muted jocularity.

"Yes, Miss Leah," he said. "I understand that you have to do your job."

"I'll talk to Chief Ben," said Leah. "We might be able to-"

Geoffrey put up a hand, gently interrupting her.

"No, Miss Leah," he said. "Because he might escape and you know I won't. I was never a strong man. But I can do this."

Leah stared at him.

"The responsibility falls to me, and I swore just like you to serve and protect," said Geoffrey. "I know you'd do the same, in my place."

"All right. I have to go," she said, standing to leave. "But let me know if you need anything?"

Geoffrey nodded.

"Of course," he said. "And Miss Leah?"

"Yes?"

"Whatever you do," he said quietly. "Don't let me run. *Promise me* you won't let me run."

Caught in his gaze, she nodded, and put a hand on the latch. "I promise," she said.

***

Later that day, Leah turned from her computer to see Dorian and Magnus enter the station together. Their eyes were now the soft seal-brown colour she had grown accustomed to. They seemed a trifle embarrassed, as though Leah having seen them in their previous state was tantamount to having seen them in a compromising position.

"Welcome back," she said.

Magnus bowed, and went to the kitchen for tea. Dorian made to follow him.

"Don't you leave, Dorian Grey," she commanded, and Dorian stood still. "You abandoned me out there, and I only had help from a vampire to take down the first serial killer in Fae history. Do you want to explain yourself?"

Dorian's dour expression was unchanged. She crossed her arms.

"You asked me what your weapons were," he said. "The curse of being magical is magic itself. The curse of being a story is that you are bound to how the story must be told. Every powerful creature has a weakness, and every creature that seems weak has untold power. We are slaves to the story, Leah Bishop, and as I have told you, the seal-folk are both blessed and cursed. There are times when we save you and there are times when you save us."

Leah shook her head. Dorian sat down beside her.

"I understand you are angry with me, Leah," he said. "You have every right to be. You are stronger and more useful than you think. You have weapons, and you are necessary to this force. You are the strongest human I know, and I am proud to have you as my partner."

Leah smiled at him despite herself.

"We Fae are often trapped by our own power," he said. "In the selkie cantrip, we are held in its thrall. Now that Sebastian has been caught, the cantrip has released us. If you hadn't been there, we would have torn him limb from limb. We are capable of destroying the world, Leah. I was not lying about that."

Leah started. Dorian held her gaze.

"It has been long since I was a killer," he said, "long since the selk walked in darkness, a ghost legion dripping with the cold of the sea, to become the horror of those people on the lonely roads, tarrying too late after pub close. It has been long since the selk raised their hand in anger against anyone. I thank you for defusing a situation I was helpless to control."

Leah was about to reply when Chief Ben approached.

"They found another body," he said.

"What?" Leah said, "but Sebastian's been arrested."

"Yes," he said. "Much like the other one, it looks as if this was done a while ago. I am hoping this will be the last one we find. You'll have to go and see Milo."

***

Leah and Dorian walked through the Labyrinth to the morgue.

The mist began to gather, obscuring her view.

Oh, no. Not again.

She found herself alone. There was a door. Leah recognised it as the door to the Minotaur's barn. She smiled a bit and decided she'd ask him for help again.

She pushed the door open and nearly fell off of a cliff.

She backed towards the door and stared around herself in

disbelief. The ocean crashed loudly against the rocks in front of her.

Leah was standing on the side of a cliff, in a manicured garden. There were fountains everywhere, little rivers and waterfalls set into the grounds. It was beautiful and desolate. There was no one else around. Mist rose from the sea and she saw, to her surprise, that there was a small pathway to a beach. There was also a feeling of intense loneliness to the place, as severe as a wound. She looked back towards the door and wondered if she should chance it just as she saw a strange, dark shape rising beneath the water. A black tentacle crept out from the sea, the waves crashing over it as it felt along the sand, and then the cliffs.

Searching. It is searching for something...

"What the-" Leah began, and yelped when she felt a strong hand on her arm.

She turned to see the Minotaur.

"Best leave now," he advised.

She looked over her shoulder and saw that the tentacle had crept over the cliff and was edging along the lawn towards them.

"Agreed," said Leah, backing into the hallway of the Labyrinth and closing the door firmly.

"You gotta be more careful," said the Minotaur. "I won't always be here. Your partner will be missing you. Go through that door. And remember, follow the directions next time."

Leah nodded, and went through the door the Minotaur indicated.

"Leah!" Dorian said. "What happened? You keep getting lost down here. It's very dangerous!"

"Sorry," said Leah. "I'm fine now."

She told him what had happened and what the Minotaur had said.

"What the hell was that, in the ocean?" she asked.

Dorian looked like he wasn't going to answer.

"Oh no," she said. "None of this cryptic mysterious crap. You know I might end up down here without you and I need to understand the dangers I might be facing. Out with it."

He studied her for a moment and then relented.

"It is a beast of the deep," he said. "There are doors upon doors underneath Caledonia. There is no end to this station that we know of, as the builders are long gone. You can access it from anywhere in the city. It spreads out beneath the entirety of Glasgow and beyond. How deep it goes, I cannot tell. No one can. You merely need to find the most incongruous-looking element of most Glasgow neighbourhoods, and run towards it. Frequently, it will be a passageway into some part of Caledonia, and as you are an officer, the doorways will recognise you. You can find yourself here in the Labyrinth, in relative safety, as long as you have your wits about you. Most of the things down here are friendly and might even be your fellow officers. We have many officers both above ground and below, in many places of the world."

Leah did not miss the implications of *most of*, but she let it slide.

"And this *beast of the deep*, what purpose does it serve?" she asked.

"Purpose?" asked Dorian, puzzled, "It just is. What purpose do you or I serve? We are. It is. The door serves as a passageway to another land."

"Another land? Like Greece or something?" she asked. "It looked Mediterranean."

"Not all doors lead to Earthly places," said Dorian.

Leah stared at him.

"I advise you to be careful about directions in the Labyrinth, and what doors you open, until you've spent more time in this world."

"Right," said Leah, full of questions that may never have answers.

Dorian shook his head, and they entered the morgue together.

Milo was there, sitting beside the corpse of a lovely young

woman. His long, golden-orange tail was soaking in a cast-iron clawfoot bathtub as he made notes while he examined the body. He looked up as they entered.

"Hello," he said. "Thanks for coming down."

"What time did she come in?" asked Dorian.

"About an hour ago," said Milo. "I'm going to start the autopsy in half an hour, but I thought you might want to have a look first."

The *ceasg* sighed.

"Not that I think the autopsy is going to tell us anything," said Milo, looking at the dead woman. "No more than the others have told us, at any rate. I'm about to admit defeat, Dorian, and you know I hate that."

"You haven't been able to find any cause of death?" asked Leah.

Milo indicated a chair beside the table and she sat down next to him.

"Nothing," he said, motioning to the body with the end of his pen. "There are no marks anywhere, same as all the others. She was not poisoned. There are only a few surefire ways to kill the Fae, but none of them are evident here. It is very puzzling. We know the killer now, but not how he killed."

Leah looked at the woman on the table and then turned to look at the lab, the creatures, the mysterious bubbling liquids, and the refrigerators that held evidence from countless cases.

"You have a morgue, though?" she asked.

Milo nodded.

"Yes," he said. "Normally, we investigate faerie crimes *against humans*. The human bodies come to us first, and then are sent to the human police afterwards. It's quite rare for us to investigate monster crimes against other monsters. These days, everyone seems to get along fairly well."

"How much do human police know about us?" asked Leah.

"Not very much," he said. "They don't know what we are, exactly. They think we are merely a specialist branch of Interpol. We rarely get visitors, and of course I can't interact with the human police."

He grinned, and indicated his tail. Then he sighed.

"I do miss Geoffrey. He was very good. I am disappointed that I didn't spot him sooner. I like to consider myself a kind of detective, too. I just investigate bodies. However, with these murders, there have been absolutely no clues. Each one of these Fae has been in near-perfect health."

"It's as if they just gave up?" asked Leah, and Milo nodded.

Leah looked down at the body of the woman. She had been very beautiful, with olive skin and curly hair, large dark eyes, and long lashes. Her long, graceful arms lay at her sides, and her manicured fingernails showed she had taken care of her appearance during her life.

Leah started. She noticed something glittering between the woman's fingers.

"Milo," she said. "What is that?"

Milo looked closely, and gently pried the woman's hand open. There was a small, teardrop-shaped glass pendant, filled with water, resting in the centre of her palm. Milo handed it to Leah.

"I don't recognise it," he said.

Dorian moved closer.

"I do," he said. "This is a selkie's tear pendant. But I haven't seen one in years. They are very old-fashioned. Sentimental. Almost foolish, really. The selkie keeps the tears of his lover next to his heart. Even *I* am not as old-fashioned as that."

"I can't imagine that ever being the case," said Leah.

Dorian smiled and took the pendant from her, studying it.

"I don't know why it would be here with this body," said Dorian, after a moment. "These tears do not belong to this woman. Believe me, I can tell."

He examined it closely.

"I can tell you what I do know from this." Dorian said. "The selkie that this pendant belonged to was Taken by a woman that a human man already loved. Seven tears into the sea. A woman disappointed in love. That is the formula. The human men are not always too pleased when they discover that the woman they love has found another man."

"I thought that the selk could only be with single women," Leah said.

"Disappointed in love doesn't always mean single," Dorian said.

"What do we do n-" Leah began, and that was when the first wave hit.

Adam walked towards her, smiling.

Leah's heart ached as though it had been seared with a branding iron. The vision disappeared as quickly as it had come.

"Are you all right?" Dorian asked, as she regained consciousness, gasping in horror.

"No," she managed, as another vision blindsided her.

She was drowning.

Adam was talking to a strange woman in a café. That was the first time she saw them together.

When she had confronted him about it, how easily he had lied.

"I don't know what you're talking about," he had said. "You're always so overdramatic and suspicious. I can't help it if women are attracted to me. It's meaningless. Stop being jealous. It's unattractive."

Leah clawed her way back to consciousness, her stomach roiling.

She opened the door to their flat, tossing her keys on the table. She rifled through the mail. Dimly, she became aware of sounds coming from the bedroom. There was knowledge there, before she had even been aware of it, a terrible sinking feeling. She knew better, but she couldn't help herself. She had to know.

She saw them together. Everything she had never wanted to be true. Every time she had doubted herself. Every time she had feared this. Adam was a liar with a beautiful face.

There was a reason Lucifer was called morning star, most beautiful. It is so very human to equate beauty with a good heart. The snake is smooth, the honest are jagged.

Leah's eyes opened and she was in the morgue again with Milo and Dorian. It was only a trough between waves, but she called out through the storm.

"It's showing me Adam," she managed to say, before she was lost beneath a sea of memory.

Leah heard a new voice, narrating, among the hurricane of images and lost days that trapped her. She recognized the voice as Geoffrey's, but with the sharpened notes of Sebastian's cold silver tongue:

You think your hearts are broken?

She was dimly aware of Dorian collapsing to the floor.

You think you have reason to fear, reason to weep, in the dark hours?

Leah saw Milo looking down at them with disinterested curiosity.

She had gone outside and sat down on the front step, in tears. She no longer cared who saw her.

And then he came outside. He had put his arms around her shoulders, talked in a soothing voice. He tried to comfort her, tried to convince her she was overreacting. The other woman was still inside, in their bed, and he was trying to tell her that she was overreacting to him shattering their lives.

How she had desired the comfort of his touch and had been repulsed by it.

How she had doubted what she had seen with her own eyes, how she knew, now, that he was a liar and not to be trusted, but how she did not quite believe it either.

She felt the desperation of loving him and the sick feeling of knowing she was wrong to do so. She was so foolish, and the other woman must have laughed at her... and still, how difficult it was to convince her mind that this man, her husband, her love, was a stranger to her now. That he was the enemy, and in many ways, had always been.

He was poison, and she had been intoxicated, unaware.

Sebastian's voice cut through this memory, harsh and furious.

How they could send the heartbroken against me, I'll never know.

The waters dragged Leah down into the black depths, where no sunlight could reach.

Adam looked at her with those beautiful eyes.

And suddenly, stronger than the pain, she remembered.

The selk stared at Sebastian, surrounding him in the evening light by the statue and the magic was strong; her heart was breaking again and again.

But Leah knew she had to escape and she saw light. The vampire was there, coaxing Sebastian away, speaking into his ear, and she saw the cracks of light in the storm, and she knew she could break the spell.

She could fight this where they could not. Permanent heartbreak was a selkie curse.

*But humans moved on, **had** to move on or die.*

Around her, the lab, Milo, Dorian, were all fading into nothingness, caught up in the storm of her mind. But, like any good sailor, she looked for the light and for the sign of calm seas, and tacking the vessel, she turned.

Leah allowed herself this one last look at him.

Adam.

He was beautiful, but he was empty, she realised, like a counterfeit antique vase. She began to see cracks appearing on his skin. She did not want to linger and see what might be waiting underneath.

"I can't stay," she told him.

His brow clouded. That was not how this memory was meant to go.

"Why? Don't you love me?" he asked.

"I do love you," Leah said. "More than anything. But I can't stay here anymore. Dorian needs me."

The sunlight refracted through the clouds, and she could see dry land ahead.

Tears shone in Adam's eyes.

"But I love you," he said.

Leah smiled sadly.

"I wish that were true," she said. "I really do, and I wish you *had been the man I thought you were, but it's time to move on."*

And the pain fell away, like it had been some kind of cocoon, and Leah was herself again, looking out through her own eyes. The pain was still there, but not in the same way it had been.

Something had changed.

Leah went to Dorian, who was still lying on the floor. His large brown eyes stared unseeing, and he was not moving.

"Dorian!" Leah said, shaking him by the shoulder. "Wake up! What happened?"

Dorian just looked at her with his large, mournful eyes.

Leah turned and looked up into the face of the merman. He hadn't moved from his original position, but had been studying them intently and writing in the notebook on his lap. He jotted down some more notes.

"Never seen anything like it," Milo said. "Interesting."

Dorian sat up and slumped against the wall.

"What?" he asked faintly.

Milo lifted the selkie's wrist and checked his pulse.

"Seems that whatever new monster Sebastian is, he preys on your memories," said the merman. "Memories of love, apparently."

Leah exchanged a glance with Dorian.

"Yes," said Dorian. "He does have that kind of magic. He was able to use our memories against us when the selk attacked him. Leah seems to have the ability to break out of it."

"How did he reach us down here?" Leah asked. "He's in a cell."

"Maybe it's related to the tear pendant," Milo shrugged. "You both touched it."

"So did you," said Leah. "You're all right, though?"

"Yes," said Milo, clicking a penlight and shining and shining into her eyes. "But my only passion is science. Secondly, I'm a merman. We're not meant to love."

He looked at her seriously, and leaned in close. Leah was startled at how terrifying he was, his wide eyes inhuman and cold.

"We'll eat your soul," he said. "But love? Love is for humans and seal-men."

He continued to stare at her until Leah nodded. He drew back, and returned to writing in his notebook.

"Lucky you," said Leah slowly, turning. "Dorian-"

He looked at her.

"Yes?"

"Do you think a selkie might be involved in this?"

***

And the rain fell.

And the sky was grey.

Summer, so it was grey forever.

Night did not come to Scotland, not in July, except for a few breaths of darkness.

And Leah lay in bed, and stared out, and up, at the grey.

Her thoughts dreamed with the clouds.

...how they could send the heartbroken against me, I'll never know...

*...they are **monsters**, just like every other foul thing in their world...*

*...we're monsters, but we're not **monsters**...*

...selkies aren't exactly fighters...

...he's just disappointed that he hasn't been Taken yet...

And her heart began to beat, with the tap of the rain against the window.

And beat faster, as clarity began to build from the clouds in her eyes.

Sebastian.

The selkies.
He wasn't angry, or racist - *speciesist*?
He was *hurt*.

...they are not the innocents you believe them to be...

...do they seem gentle to you? Beautiful...

He called them *beautiful*.
So did she, of course.
Well, one in particular.
That smile, those eyes.
Self-assurance. Beauty.
Real *beauty*.
Evil is not monsters, the shadowed alleyway, the bright of a knife.
Evil is banal. It is beautiful. It is where you least expect to find it.
It is the smile of a friend with a lie on their lips.
Lucifer was called *most beautiful*.

And she remembered where she had learned that lesson, once before.

Leah sat up in her bed, slowly. The wind began to rattle the windows, as storms and violence came to Glasgow regardless of the season, and paint the sky and city grey with longing and loneliness.
Something had broken Sebastian's heart.
A man who was also Geoffrey, and might have loved her.
A folklorist knows one thing, and that is the way a story is built, and the way magic binds it, surrounds it, and gives it strength.
The Fae believe that they are all bound to the story.
That they must follow the rules of their legend.
But a human knows that stories don't always stay within the

margins.

Someone had broken out of their story and was bleeding all over the page.

Chapter Fifteen

eah and Dorian returned to Caledonia Interpol late that evening.

Chief Ben was standing next to the large arched window, staring out at the rain and the orange glow of the street lamps. He turned as they walked in.

"So, what did you find out?" he asked, folding his arms.

"I must admit, I am lost," said Dorian. "Sebastian seems to have been using an enchanted selkie's tear pendant, but for what reason I cannot imagine. He has some kind of magic. He used our memories against us, Chief. I have no idea if he sold his soul or is in league with a wizard. I do not know what to do next."

"I have a suggestion," Leah said.

They turned to look at her.

"Which is?" asked Chief Ben.

"Magnus," Leah said.

"Magnus?" asked Dorian. "Why? He's half-crazed with grief and rage, the way only a selkie can be. He's useless to us."

"If you believe that Sebastian murdered Hazel," said Leah, "I think we should talk to him about that."

"Sorry, Leah, but I agree with Dorian," said Chief Ben. "He's completely useless right now, and I don't see how he could help."

"I think that Magnus knows more than he is letting on," Leah said. "You said that Sebastian's activity only became apparent *after* Hazel's death. That makes it sound as if the two things are related. I think we should talk to him. I get the feeling that he's hiding something."

Dorian stared at Leah for a moment, considering this.

"Lies are forbidden among our people," he said.

"But you are *capable* of lying, right?" she asked.

"Yes," said Ben. "Or they would not have the reputation they have as the Don Juans of the faerie world."

Dorian pressed his lips together at this comment, but said nothing.

"I can't imagine why Magnus would lie," he said.

"Well, let's ask him," Leah replied.

***

They found Magnus at the Crystal Palace, drinking down some kind of vinegar wine. The gorgeous building was more attractive than a Wetherspoon's chain pub had a right to be, and for wine that cost £5 a bottle, it really couldn't be beat. Glaswegians will drink at whatever time of day, and anything with the label 'alcohol' will do.

Magnus was in fine form this afternoon. He was seated next to one of the floor-to-ceiling windows, the sunlight illuminating his angelic features. Leah surreptitiously looked around the room to see if anyone else had noticed the glowing man basking in the late afternoon sun, but no one seemed interested. She thought that the way Magnus was shining like a beacon would be noticeable to others, but perhaps her manual was correct, and humans really didn't notice what they didn't want to see, or didn't believe was there.

The day was surprisingly sunny, especially considering what Leah was about to do.

Glasgow's undependable weather was predictable only in the sense that it would probably be the opposite of what you were looking for. A tragedy in sunlight, a love story in the wind and rain-soaked damp.

Magnus looked up, the sunlight casting shadows over his perfect cheekbones and illuminating every facet of his extraordinary eyes, brilliant and hard. Leah glanced at Dorian and noted that his eyes were the same. She wondered if their human lovers had known immediately that they were more than human.

Unfortunately, she had a feeling that what she needed to do now was a part of the job she would never get used to.

"Hello," said Magnus, smiling up at them. "What's going on?"

"We need to ask you some questions," Leah told him.

She was only going on a hunch. She realised that if she was wrong, she would be incurring the wrath of an ancient, incredibly powerful faerie race whose capacity for vengeance went far beyond the love and beauty they so frequently professed as their reason for being.

Still. *Here goes nothing.*

She took a deep breath.

"Magnus, did your lover belong to Sebastian?" Leah asked.

Magnus's black-brown eyes grew even brighter, if that were possible.

"Yes," he said slowly. "But that is normal for a selkie. If a woman is unhappy, she cries seven tears into the sea and a selkie man comes for her."

"I know the lore," she told him. "I've been studying it my whole life. My question is, did she or did she not, *actually* cry the seven tears into the sea, Magnus?"

Dorian's mouth dropped open. He turned to look at his partner.

"I certainly hope that you are aware of the seriousness of this accusation," he told her.

"Yes, Dorian, but the selk become men in human form," she said. "And a human man can fall in unrequited love. And a human man with supernatural powers could use those powers to bewitch a woman away from her husband."

"I will not listen to this!" Dorian shouted, startling the neds and other honourable patrons of the Crystal Palace. "Magnus, tell her you would *never* do that! That the selk would never do that. It would be a terrible, twisted abuse of our powers."

"Dorian," Magnus said softly. "Be quiet. She's right."

Dorian turned from Leah slowly, looking at his brother in disbelief.

"Magnus," he said. He could say nothing more.

Magnus sighed, and looked out the window.

"Sebastian's wife, Hazel, was the most beautiful human I have ever laid eyes on," he said. "She was graceful, talented, cultured and sophisticated. She reminded me of the women from so long ago that maybe only Dorian and I can remember them now. Sebastian wasn't good enough for her. He had no money, he wanted to curse her with the dull existence of an archaeologist's wife. What kind of life was that for a woman like Hazel?"

"She loved him, though. And he loved her, right?" Leah asked.

Magnus stared at the table.

"Yes," he said, even more quietly. "There was nothing I could do. No matter how often we talked, she remained dedicated to Sebastian, and he to her. I just knew that it was *wrong*, I knew that she shouldn't be with him. I was desperately, hopelessly in love. I wanted her to go to the sea, to cry the tears. I told her the legends, over and over. She thought me funny, charming, full of old folktales."

He swallowed. His eyes darkened.

"She called me her *best friend*."

Leah rolled her eyes.

"But you managed to do it, to make her fall in love with you," she said. "How?"

Magnus looked at them. Dorian's eyes were filled with tears. Leah had never seen him look so betrayed. She felt for him, but this was the job. It needed to be done.

"I used the selkie charm," he confessed. "I used our power to bewitch her."

"That is dark magic!" Dorian burst out. "No selkie is permitted to do that! Ever!"

"Dark magic?" Leah asked. "What does that mean? Why have power that no one can use?"

Dorian looked at her in agony.

"The selkie folk, like any other faerie people, are divided into the Seelie and Unseelie Courts," he explained.

"The good and evil faeries," Leah agreed. "But I would assume that the selk were members of the Seelie court?"

"For the most part, we are," he said. "But like all kind-hearted faeries, we have a dark side, power we are capable of if pushed too far. You saw the power we have over the weather. That has not always been used for good."

"And why haven't the courts made it impossible to use that power?" Leah asked.

"Why do some people carry knives?" he asked. "Sometimes a dangerous weapon is necessary. But to do this, to use it for your own gain, it is unbelievable."

Dorian's disgust towards such an abuse was so strong that he could barely speak. His own brother, a selkie himself, becoming what the selk hated most in the world, there was no human equivalent. The closest comparison would be finding out that a member of their family was a particularly horrific serial killer.

Leah watched Dorian carefully. She reminded herself that the Victorian British conquered nations and built an empire so vast the sun never set.

"Tell us the story," she said, pulling up a chair and indicating that Dorian should join her. "We've got all the time in the world."

After a moment, his eyes never leaving his brother's, Dorian sat down beside his partner as Magnus began to explain.

London, England
1968

It was the height of the 1960s.

The UK was swinging, the Beatles were on the charts.

Magnus was seated in the café area of a glass and aluminium building in King's Road, Chelsea.

It was midsummer, and the shop had only just opened. It offered records, a chemist's, and an old-fashioned soda fountain. The place would soon become known as the infamous Chelsea Drugstore.

Magnus had found that his long hair and beautiful features were 'in' again, and he was enjoying himself immensely. The sixties were a selkie's dream, everything and everyone free; sex, drugs, music. For Magnus, it was a candy store of delights.

He saw her walk in, her black hair framing her face. She wore round white sunglasses and a bright yellow dress with white go-go boots that clacked across the cloverleaf design on the tile floor. She took off her sunglasses to reveal large, dark eyes framed with long lashes, and she ordered a dandelion and burdock soda.

Magnus was captivated.

She turned then, and saw him. He smiled, that soft and gentle smile that had bedded countless women over the centuries. She saw the leather bound journal on the table, the quill pen in his hand, and the beautiful hair in carefully arranged curls tumbling over one shoulder. He could not have dressed the part of the romantic poet more perfectly. To his surprise, she addressed him first.

"If I didn't know any better," she said, "I'd think you were a hippie. Though looking at your clothes and your hair, there aren't many hippies that can afford an entire outfit by Ossie Clark, or know how to care for their curls the way you do."

Magnus bowed slightly.

"Well spotted," he said. "I'm Magnus Grey."

"Hazel Worthington," she said, removing a white glove to shake his hand. "Beautifully manicured nails, too. What do you do?"

"I'm a model," he said.

"What a coincidence," she replied. "I'm a designer."

"That explains your ability to recognise the cut of my clothes."

"Everyone who's anyone knows of Clark. Do you mind if I sit with you?"

Magnus's grin widened.

"By all means, please do," he said, and they spent a long afternoon in conversation.

Magnus walked home that night with her telephone number in his pocket, and his heart filled with the foreign sentiment of love. Was this what being Taken was like? He didn't think so. She hadn't called for him. This felt to him like a hunger, an addiction he could not sate no matter how often he saw her or spoke with her.

Over the months that passed, he and Hazel became close, but she never seemed to respond to any of his advances. He kept his love secret. He had never felt this way, and in the past his conquests were simple, because they had only been conquests.

He had never wanted anything more than he wanted Hazel Worthington.

He was confused. He thought the selk could only fall in love if the tears were wept into the sea, and Hazel was not an unhappy woman. Quite the contrary, in fact.

One night, she attended a party at Magnus's flat. Everyone was there, other models, starlets, celebrities. His friend Sebastian, a rather nerdy type who worked at the Institute, had also attended, but he never did well at parties. Magnus was Sebastian's best friend, although they rarely saw each other. They met years before, when Magnus needed help on a case. Those employed by Caledonia Interpol couldn't talk about it freely among humans, of course, so everyone had a cover story. Magnus modelled part-time; he loved the money, the jet-set crowd, and of course the compliment to his vanity, but he would always be a police officer first.

"Who's this, Magnus?" Hazel had asked him, when she noticed Sebastian sitting uncomfortably on the sofa.

"Oh, you haven't met?" said Magnus. "Hazel Worthington, this is Sebastian Bloodworth."

Sebastian stood up, flustered, and shook her hand.

"Sebastian Bloodworth!" said Hazel. "What a name! Like something out of James Bond. Sexy."

Sebastian blushed to the roots of his hair.

"Oh, well, I wouldn't say that," he stammered.

"Can I get either of you a drink?" asked Magnus.

"Please," she said. "I'd love a glass of champagne. Thank you, Magnus."

When he left, it had never occurred to him that she might find

Sebastian attractive. He was the British librarian type, all stutters, v-neck jumpers, and emotional repression. He was the most unfashionable man imaginable, a holdover from the fifties: black and white, not Technicolor. In an era like the sixties, such a man was generally invisible to all women.

Magnus returned with two glasses of champagne in his hand, only to find his friend deep in conversation with Hazel. To his surprise, and growing horror, she seemed to be responding to Sebastian in a way she never had to him. Eventually it became obvious that Magnus was an unwelcome third party and he excused himself. He had gone off the celebration, and went to brood alone on his balcony overlooking the city.

He was not surprised, after a few weeks had passed, to discover that Sebastian and Hazel had become an item. Hazel told him herself, since she considered him her best friend.

Magnus was filled with consternation. He looked at his beautiful face in the mirror, his perfect hair, his admirable body. He was a poet, he could speak countless languages, he was eternal, and he was magic. How could Hazel prefer a man like Sebastian over a man like him?

His desperation increased, as he tried to tell her what he was, by telling her every story of the seal-people he could think of, every glamour of Faerie, every possible thing to charm her away from Sebastian. He even took her to Paris, and showed her his favourite haunts, the secret restaurants and wine cellars of the city. His fortune was boundless, he could grant her every wish.

One night while they were in Paris, he found her on the balcony, looking across the city. He approached her, wishing with every fibre of his being to touch her, to put his arms around her, to claim her as his own. By this point, Magnus had been driven mad by his longing, and by her silent refusal.

"What is it?" asked Magnus.

She turned to look at him, smiled, and sighed.

"Oh, Magnus," she said. "You've always been so wonderful to me. You've been my best friend for a long time, and I can't express how amazing it is to be here in Paris with you. It was such a sur-

prise. You know I've wanted to come here for years."

"But..." he asked.

Hazel smiled.

"But people change. Dreams change. Here I am, in the city of lights," she said, "and all I can think about is going home. I look out across this city, and I think of the sea that separates me from him. I feel it, that distance, like a physical pain."

She laughed then, a musical sound.

"Oh, listen to me!" she said. "I sound like a silly girl. You do understand, though, don't you? You were always so keen on romance."

Magnus's teeth ground together, as he tried to keep his expression placid and gentle.

"Yes," he said. "I think I understand too well."

She left Paris in the morning, and Magnus returned the following week.

They never spoke of the trip again.

In six months, Hazel and Sebastian were married.

Sebastian asked Magnus to be his best man as he was the best friend of both the bride and groom. He attended the wedding in the finery of the seal-folk, a coat of woven gold. He was the most splendid person there, but everyone saw only Hazel, and the radiance of her happiness. When she said **I do**, he nearly passed out. When they kissed, he looked away. Afterwards, she embraced Magnus, while Sebastian looked on, smiling happily.

Magnus envied him, the happiest man in the world. Sebastian was so innocent and naïve, he couldn't have suspected the evil coursing through the veins of his best friend, driven to madness by these new sensations of love and rejection.

Over the course of Magnus's friendship with Hazel, whenever she had broken up with someone, she would spend the night at his flat. They would share a bottle of wine, and she would weep. He would comfort her. As he held her and wiped away her tears, he would carefully collect them and counted seven into a vial, in secret.

Since she met Sebastian, Hazel hadn't wept. Magnus did not use the tears because he still hoped she would one day see the light, and come to him. But an unconscious practicality made him keep them nearby, just in case.

As their blissful marriage passed from weeks into months, hatred poisoned his yearning. He could no longer stand it. He put the pendant around his neck and spoke the cantrip meant only for the salvation of those who needed it. A secret spell meant to charm the abused from their abusers, the most guarded of all the selkie powers.

It was a matter of weeks before Hazel left Sebastian. She had called Magnus and told him that she could not stop thinking of him day or night, and that she was unable to sleep. She had confessed her sudden love for Magnus to Sebastian in tears, and he had accepted it in silence. While rejection was unfamiliar to Magnus, to Sebastian it was like an old friend. He watched her pack her things, and only said he felt blessed to have been able to share her life and joys with her for as long as he had. Blinking back tears, he said that her memory would always be looked upon with fondness.

Magnus was thrilled. He brazenly met Hazel at the door of Sebastian's flat, and without a word or even a look to his friend, accompanied her to their new life together. Sebastian, wordless and broken, had watched her walk away. Not only had she left him, his best friend had betrayed him.

Still, Sebastian loved them both, and he wanted them to be happy. He was a quiet, unassuming man, and believed only the best of people.

Over the moon, Magnus showered Hazel with gifts, took her out to the best restaurants, wined and dined her as only a selkie knew how. Things were not all that they seemed, unfortunately.

During the night, she would say Sebastian's name again and again in her sleep, and wake, confused, to find herself with Magnus. Those nights, she wouldn't go anywhere near him. Day after day, she seemed happy, only to suddenly seem puzzled, as if she were half-waking from a dream.

❧ Chapter Fifteen ❧

Sebastian's name was never far from her lips, and the faraway look in her eyes drove Magnus to despair. It seemed that she would never truly be his.

One morning, he awoke to find a note on the bedside table. With trembling hands, he lifted it, and read:

Dear Magnus, you have always been my best friend, and I love you dearly. However, I can't love you as I love Sebastian. I feel that I have made a terrible mistake, and I am going to correct it, if I can. I am so sorry, and I hope you will forgive me. I wish you all the best, and perhaps when things have settled, we can speak again. For now, I ask that you respect me, and to honour your love for me, by keeping your distance.
Love, Hazel.

Magnus's breath started to come in short gasps, and he crushed the note in his hand as if he could overcome what she had said with the sheer power of the ancient race that had bore him.

She had been able to break the bond and walk away.

Magnus looked around himself, at his enormous flat with its built-in bar, his hi-fi system, the loft, and the balcony overlooking the city. He had everything, and it was all hollow and silent.

It did not take him long to find himself at the door to Hazel and Sebastian's flat.

His eyes were mad, and wild, and blazing ice blue, with centuries of storm and sea. Hazel had no time to run or cry out. He stabbed her again and again, his hand tight around a silver knife slick with blood, and he wept, sobbing incoherently as the bottle she was holding smashed across the floor and mixed red wine with thick blood that pooled onto the white tiles. Hazel collapsed, and upon falling, saw the sunlight through the window glint off of the glass tear pendant that swung from Magnus's chest. With weak hands she snatched at it, snapping the chain.

Magnus looked down one last time at her shattered frame, and then stared at his hands, at the blood, the life taken by them. They were soft and supple, meant to be offered as a gentleman's prayer, to help, to protect, to lend succour, to be trusted. These hands, only meant to be offered in support, had destroyed the only human he had ever loved.

He stood, and opened the door with a dead calm he did not recognise. Once outside, the guilt began to wash over him, and his thoughts were only of escape. He vaulted over the wall and ran as far and fast as he could go.

No one saw him. In the darkness, he buried the knife and his clothing deep in a field near an overpass where he himself would never again be able to find them. Sobbing, desperate, he disappeared into the night.

Chapter Sixteen

So, if you couldn't have her, no one could," Leah said as Magnus finished, hating herself for knowing exactly what that kind of anger felt like.

Magnus didn't respond.

"You killed the others, didn't you?" she asked. "You were the first Fae serial killer and so you killed the humans that belonged to the other selk? You wanted to draw suspicion away from yourself, and the fae believed that only humans were serial killers. *The selk just don't do that kind of thing.*"

"*Magnus?!*" Dorian cried.

"She's right, Dorian," said Magnus coldly. "I don't understand how she knows, but she's right."

Dorian looked absolutely miserable.

"We will tell the selk," said Leah.

This was the first time Magnus's serene countenance was shaken.

"You cannot tell them!" he said. "The selk won't hunt me, they will turn their backs. I would be exiled!"

"It is already done," said Dorian, "Such is the way of our people."

"There are worse things in this world than them knowing," said Leah.

***

The mood at Caledonia was one of muted sadness. They had lost two of their own, traitors in their midst. It did not reflect well on the force, or on the Fae in general.

What happens when monsters try to change? To live an honest life? Some things are beyond even their power or comprehension.

Magnus hadn't spoken since his arrest. Leah had put him into one of the cells, magic holding him in place. He had gone quietly, accepting his fate. Chief Ben had informed her that he would need to be transported to the Fae Council to await his trial. Soon, he would be put in the maximum security cells, located in the Deeps of Caledonia Interpol.

The door to the cell block opened. Magnus lifted his head.

Dorian entered, walking down the rows of cells until he reached Magnus's and saw, to his surprise, that his brother had been weeping. In all his long life, he did not remember his brother often shedding tears.

Dorian recognised that Magnus had a selkie heart like his own. For decades he had wondered if Magnus was even a member of the same species, but now he realised that Magnus felt love more keenly than he had expected and it had driven him insane. Dorian hid his own heart with a stiff upper lip, and Magnus with abandon and vulgarity.

Now, for different reasons, they both were questioning the wisdom of leaving the ocean so long ago.

Dorian sat down and leaned back against the glass wall outside Magnus's cell. His brother moved towards him, leaning against the other side, so they were bookends, one golden and angelic, the other dark and pale.

"Do you remember," Dorian said softly, "when we were young, and diving the shoals? The silver flashes of fish, the green darkness that wrapped around us and held us safe from this human world?"

Magnus's head was bowed. He looked down at his hands.

"Yes," he said. "I remember."

Dorian spread his white hands wide. He looked at his long slender fingers, perfectly shaped and delicate.

"We came here, to the land, you and I, together," he said. "We left the sea, our home, and cold-bellied, in the darkness, worked our way onto the sand. In the moonlight, the sealskin fell away from our human forms, large eyes and dark lashes all that was left of our former lives, and we glistened in the silver light like the white of waves on the shore."

He looked down at his clothes, at the form of his perfect legs, and turned to see his dull reflection in the glass of the cell, the sweep of his impossibly white cheekbone to long lashes and animal eyes.

Magnus turned to look at him.

"What a strange life we found it, did we not?" Dorian asked. "These long limbs, these legs for running swiftly, feeling wind that for the first time was not from a storm-tossed sea. Rain streaming through our hair, across our human bodies.

'We were beautiful, Magnus. We *are* beautiful.

'And we are pain. We are the truth woven through this world. Help me to understand, brother, because I do not think I can. And if I cannot understand, I cannot forgive you."

Magnus looked at his own body, so much more powerful than his brother's delicate frame and sharp features. His facial features were soft, almost feline, but his arms were strong, his hands masculine and lovely. His long curls were the dream of artists from Rembrandt to Botticelli. His fine muscles worked beneath his clothing, and he was then aware of all that made him human.

"Better to have kept to the sea," he laughed quietly. "Better to never have felt it, Dorian. You mention pain. I could not suffer it. When she was not with me, I was tortured, aflame. When she left me, when she chose him instead, it was as if some phantom force had torn my insides out through my mouth. The times you speak of, the simple joys as a seal, sporting in the waves, they were times of happiness. The delicious feeling of humanity, over the centuries, the battles where we could not die, the women and wine, before she came into my life... oh, Dorian, had I known what it was to suffer the pangs of unrequited love, I should never have left that moonlit shore."

Dorian eyed him strangely.

"You are a selkie," he said. "Suffering is our purpose. We care for humankind. We are their servants, and their saviours."

"Humankind!" cried Magnus. "Thankless, and wounding! She saw my pain and she would not comfort it. She held the cure in her own hands and *she let me suffer anyway*. We save them every day and they do not know. If they knew, they would not care."

His fists were clenched against the cool stone floor of the cell. Dorian stared at his brother, his eyes cold.

"She owed you nothing, Magnus," he said. "She trusted you. She even loved you, in her way. She owed you *nothing*."

"I thought, I thought when she died, the pain would leave me," Magnus said. "I was wild, and I wanted to save others from suffering. We are all selk, and I hadn't known of the horrible pain before. I did not know how deeply it hurt. I wanted to save us all. I killed them, Dorian, I killed her, to save us this pain, but the pain is still here."

Furiously, he tore at his chest.

"*The pain is still here!*" he shouted. "I curse this selkie heart! How can the pain still live in me? Why won't it leave me alone?"

Sobbing, he collapsed onto the floor of his cell. Dorian's jaw tightened until his teeth ground together. He turned and inflicted a cold steel gaze upon his brother's crumpled form.

"Would you have killed Dahlia?" he whispered. "Would you have killed the human I belonged to, Magnus?"

Gasping and coughing through his sobs, Magnus turned bright black eyes on his brother. He crept to the window that separated them and put his palm flat against it, his long curls falling forward. He stared into Dorian's eyes; two creatures of ethereal, impossible beauty gazing at each other through the glass.

"Oh, Dorian," Magnus said. "You are my brother, and I love you so much. *I would have killed her first.*"

Slowly, Dorian stood up and turned away. He could hear his own heartbeat in his ears, wild sea waves pounding against an unrelenting shore. Wordless, he left his brother staring after him from the hard, cold floor of the cell.

✸ CHAPTER SIXTEEN ✸

***

"Leah," Chief Ben said. "I've just received word. It's time."

Leah nodded, and went down into the cell block. She opened the door of Magnus's cell and put the handcuffs on him. He did not protest, staring off into the distance. It seemed that he was in his own world, far away, perhaps in the days of his youth when he and Dorian had no other worry than the salt of the sea and basking on the shoreline. For a moment, he paused. He looked at her, but said nothing. She pushed him gently into the corridor and he went calmly enough.

As he was led past the darkened cells, a figure emerged in one of them. Brilliant blue eyes stared out with hatred as Sebastian struck the glass.

"Did you feel her dying, you bastard?!" he cried, slamming his hands in futile fury against the cell window. "Did you hear her call my name?!"

Magnus held Sebastian's gaze with a lifeless expression. This time, Leah pushed Magnus hard, away from the cell. Sebastian scrabbled against the glass as if he might rend it with his fingernails.

"*Did you?!*" he screamed after them in anguish.

His voice caught in his throat, and this feared criminal, consumed by grief and hate, broke down into dirty, retching sobs that echoed throughout the lonely block of cells.

Chapter Seventeen

The sun was bright on Glasgow Green, and Aonghas stood with Dylan in the midst of a manicured lawn. Morning mist covered the ground, dissipating in the warmth of daylight.

"Well," said Aonghas, "this is where you are stationed. You won't feel cold, or heat, or age. You might get bored, though. And Dylan... "

"Aye?" he said.

"I'm going to have to train you."

Dylan laughed.

"Wit? You train me?" he said, "You couldnae magic yir way out o' a paper bag."

Aonghas crossed his arms.

"I know you don't like me very much," he said, "but there's a lot I can teach you. Anyway, I'm the only Guardian who's willing."

"Aye, wull," said Dylan. "You canna be all tha' bad if you helped Tearlach."

He noticed that Aonghas was holding a strange triangular wooden box.

"Wit's tha'?" he asked.

"A box," said Aonghas. "Dorian said that the police station has had it for centuries, and he knows the reason now."

Dylan saw the insignia on the side. He looked up at Aonghas.

"It's from Tearlach," Aonghas said.

Taking it, Dylan sat down on the ground immediately and prised the box open.

The box was full of folded paper, brown with age. He realised they were letters. Stunned, he lifted the first, and unfolded it.

My dearest Dylan. I've met a young lady, I think you would like her. Beautiful long hair and she knows how to fight, which is a blessing in my time...

and the next -

Dear Dylan, my son has turned one this year. I named him after you, of course.

My dear friend, today I met Bonnie Prince Charlie. He is not as bonnie as his reputation says, and has no head for drink...

Dear Dylan, I am turning sixty-five. It seems that in all my long life I shall never age to a time when we will meet again. I look forward to your visit, should you make one.

Dylan, old friend and companion, I have written you for many years, as promised. I only hope that you'll receive my letters. They say that I have a condition, and will be gone within a year...

Dylan. They say it will be soon. I tell them I know that we will meet again, and they think me mad. I'll never forget your friendship and your strange ways, your interesting food and how you watched over me. Mourn me not, friend and brother. Know that I have loved you, and keep well. My thoughts and prayers are with you, always.
-Tearlach.

Dylan dug through the box, but there were no more letters. He could barely breathe.

"I hafta go t' him!" he cried in anguish.

Aonghas reached over and pulled him into a hug. This time, Dylan did not push him away.

"He's had a good life, Dylan," Aonghas said gently. "You were a wonderful story and an inspiration to him. A comfort in his last hours. Let it be."

Dylan let out a breath. He nodded, and smiled. He lifted every letter in the box, and held them to his chest as if he could embrace his friend through all that distance.

***

Dorian and Leah met Milo in the lab, where he was testing the necklace and its contents.

Leah examined the pendant. It was made of blown glass in a teardrop design. A tiny amount of water was sealed inside, with an ornate pewter decorative seal and a loop for the string.

A symbol of love, twisted into one of loss and revenge.

"So this was how Sebastian killed the Fae?" she asked.

Milo nodded.

"Yes," he said. "When they touched it, they were drowned in their memories, overwhelmed. Every one of these creatures had loved someone or something so deeply that they simply gave up hope. They chose to end rather than suffer. You are strong, Leah Bishop. You have survived Sebastian's magic twice now."

Dorian looked pensive, and far away. He hadn't spoken much since Magnus had been transferred.

"Then they committed suicide," Dorian mused. "They weren't killed."

Milo splashed some water onto the floor with his tail as he adjusted his position in the bath.

"A technicality," he said. "They chose to die, yes. But without Sebastian's power, his intervention, they would still be alive. What do you want to do about this?"

"It's *Sebastian*," said Dorian. "I think the Fae Court would like to put him on the stand and give him a fair trial, if not for the murders, then for his other crimes against the supernaturals. He has worked with criminals, both supernatural and human, over the years - smuggling, corporate crime, anything to climb to the top of the criminal element of the city. Murder had never been a part of his repertoire in the past, and it seems as if it will not occur again. However, this is not his first offence, and it won't be his last. He may not have killed these Fae with his own two hands, but he certainly meant for them to die. And for what? To prove a point? To reveal who Magnus truly was? Why didn't he just come out and tell us? Or why didn't he kill Magnus, come to that?"

"He was afraid, Dorian," said Milo, "and remember? He hates us. He doesn't think we deserve to live, and he fears us too. He wanted revenge, and Magnus couldn't suffer if he wasn't living."

"There was *no reason* for him to do this," said Dorian, gesturing toward the freezers that held the bodies of the Fae.

"Since when is murder reasonable?" asked Leah. "Are we going to be able to prosecute, Milo? Do we have the necessary evidence to use against Sebastian?"

The merman shrugged.

"It's difficult to say," he said. "Magnus will certainly be prosecuted."

"Sebastian should also answer for his other crimes," said Dorian.

"I fear that is not going to happen," said Milo, "at least not this time. There's nothing solid we can really hold him on. This is what you might call *the perfect murder*. You might have something of a case, but it would be very hard to argue, despite Sebastian's fame in the faerie world."

"More solid than killing faeries?" demanded Dorian. "This is absolute madness, Milo, and you know it."

"Of course it is," Milo replied. "That is probably why he chose this method. He waited a very long time, Dorian, and he is extremely clever. I'm surprised he allowed himself to get caught."

"Didn't Magnus ever see Geoffrey?" asked Leah. "You'd think they'd have recognised each other."

"No," said Dorian. "Magnus developed a particular revulsion for death. Only recently, of course. Now I know why. So he never came down to the morgue. He knew, I think, when he passed Geoffrey when leaving the flat. That was the first time they had ever seen each other. It also explains why the selkie cantrip happened that day. Magnus called the selk."

Dorian sighed, and sat down in a chair beside Milo. He put his head in his hands, pulling on his black hair with his white fingertips. Leah leaned back against the wall and crossed her arms.

"I am reclaiming this," Dorian said, reaching for the pendant, "as the personal effects of Magnus Grey. There's nothing more we can do, and I would be glad to know it was somewhere no one else could ever use it."

Milo sighed deeply.

"Very well," he said, "but you'll have to answer to Chief Ben for it. That pendant is evidence against Sebastian's crimes."

"I will take good care of it," Dorian promised, and pocketed the necklace.

Leah looked at him curiously.

"Well," said Dorian, "shall we? It's been a long night for all of us, and I think we need some sleep."

"After you," said Leah, and they left Milo alone in the morgue.

Chapter Eighteen

The following morning dawned bright and clear, and Leah's usual meandering path to the station took a bit longer than necessary. She had a great deal on her mind. She walked down the darkened stairs into the faerie light, now so familiar to her, waited as the world twisted, and then walked out of the cupboard into the kitchen. She yawned, rubbing her eyes, and set the kettle to boiling. She leafed through the Metro newspaper as the kettle roared to life behind her. Chief Ben walked in, looking haggard as usual, his black leather coat creaking as he folded his arms.

"I don't know how to tell you this," he said.

Without looking up from the paper, Leah nodded.

"Sebastian's escaped," she said.

"How did you know?" he asked.

"Lucky guess. He strikes me as the type who'd have an escape plan, if he allowed himself to get caught. He infiltrated Caledonia well enough that he was able to leave a note on your desk without anyone noticing. There's no telling who or what he might have working on his side, here at Interpol. Besides, I was there. I saw how he screamed at Magnus. I think he wants to be anywhere Magnus isn't."

"Magnus isn't here anymore," said Chief Ben, "but he wouldn't know that. Sebastian can't get far, now that we know what he looks like. We'll catch him again."

"Maybe someday," she agreed absently.

Ben looked at her, exasperated.

"All right, get out," he said. "You have work to do."

She looked at him, open-mouthed, and then at the kettle ready-boiled, and down at the newspaper. She sighed and walked out of the kitchen.

Grinning to himself, Chief Ben made a cup of tea and began to leaf through the Metro.

"Dorian Grey!" Leah announced, as she walked into the library, and Dorian nearly dropped his laptop. He settled immediately. It was unseemly for a Victorian gentleman to be startled.

"Yes, Leah, what is it?" he asked.

"You need to join me," she said, "on an important mission."

Dorian was at her side in an instant.

"Lead on," he said. "What is it? What's happened?"

***

Dorian looked around the garish red coffee-shop with distrust. It was the shop located within the old subway station, the castle-like building that served as the city centre's doorway into Caledonia Interpol.

Leah sighed and leaned back in her soft armchair, holding an enormous mug of tea in her cupped hands. Steam rose from the mug and she closed her eyes, inhaled, and took a sip. She smiled.

"*This* was your emergency?" he sniffed. "Really, Miss Bishop. We ought to be working."

"Ben stole my Metro," she said loftily. "I stole his selkie. Drink your espresso. Lighten up, partner. We deserve a holiday."

Dorian raised an eyebrow. He grudgingly took a sip, and found it excellent. Perhaps there was time for some relaxation, after all. Leah grinned as he settled back into his chair. She was taking a sip of her tea when he spoke, and she had grown so accustomed to the silence that he startled her.

"I am sorry," he said suddenly.

"What for?" Leah asked.

"For not suspecting. For not realizing. For not even considering that a selkie might be capable of something like what Magnus has done."

He was crestfallen, and she heard what he meant: *I never could have imagined that it would be my brother.*

She gave him a grim look and set her mug into its saucer.

"In the last couple of years, I have learned some hard lessons," she said. "People that you have always assumed were good may not be. Some of the things you said about Magnus, and Hazel, and Sebastian didn't add up to the whole that you had always assumed was there. That's what led me to think of Magnus, as possibly keeping a secret that no one knew about. I was working off a theory, particularly one that involved knowing that you would never have suspected him. You were too close.

'I've learned that people can change for the worse, or perhaps had never been what you'd assumed they were. Hopefully the people you think you know truly are who you think they are, but that is not always the case. When they turn out to be something different, your world turns upside down and you doubt everything, everyone, even your own senses. Where other people wouldn't see it, maybe someone like me would - the heartbroken. The people the selk are so wired to protect."

"So you might have turned out like Sebastian?" he asked.

She looked hard at Dorian.

"The difference between me and Sebastian is that I'm not insane. Probably a drunk, probably obsessive, probably have a hard time letting go... but I'm not insane."

Dorian's face was paler than usual, and tears brimmed in his eyes.

"How do you stand it?" he asked. "Humans, I mean. The pain. I always thought it was the selkie's fate to suffer. I never thought it would drive one of us mad."

She smiled.

"We don't," Leah told him. "I've often wondered how you can stand losing your love, if the selk feel the same pain forever."

Dorian smiled ruefully.

"It is a beautiful pain," he said, "and what we were built for. This, I have no frame of reference for."

"Magnus is your brother," Leah said. "It's a different kind of love."

"So we have two firsts," said Dorian sadly. "The first Fae serial killer, and the first serial killer of the Fae."

Leah nodded, taking a drink of her tea.

"There's still one more problem, come to that," he said, businesslike again.

"What's that?"

"We still need to find Sebastian," he replied.

Leah's mobile phone began to ring. She picked it up.

"Hello?" she asked.

"Ah, Miss Bishop," said a silver voice she knew too well. "Geoffrey sends his regards."

"Sebastian," she said, waving at Dorian. He looked sharply at her.

"Your memory serves you well."

"Where are you?" she asked.

He laughed, a cold, hollow sound.

"Now, really," he said, "I thought you were a clever girl."

"We'll find you-"

"Yes, yes. All in good time," he said. "You and the Amazing Seal Boy. I will watch your career with *interest*. This is not, unfortunately, a call for pleasure."

Leah shot Dorian a look.

"Yes, I committed the murders. There, you have a confession. Well done," said Sebastian. "I think you've earned my statement, considering that you did indeed arrest Mr. Grey. The point is, Miss Leah - as Geoffrey so liked to call you - I'm not the important thing here."

"No? You don't think so?" Leah demanded. "The first serial killer of faeries?"

"Oh come now. Serial killer? How *film noir*. I'm hurt," he said. "It took *you* to discover the pendant. If Milo had noticed it, perhaps there would have been fewer deaths. As it was, I was always in the perfect place to remove the pendant before he noticed, in order to give it to the next victim. But no, Leah. You *know* I did this, that's not much of a mystery. Finding out that one of the gentle selk is a monster, now that *is* news. I'm dog bites man, Leah. But Magnus, *that's* man bites dog. We're getting off the subject. The question is, why was Dylan called?"

"Called?" she asked. "I don't understand."

"Dylan," he said, exasperated. "Your ned angel. A Guardian isn't called unless the former Guardian is dead. I know you were busy trying to deal with me but you've solved the case now. Congratulations."

There was a brief pause. Leah wondered if he had hung up just as he spoke again.

"Glasgow is *my* city," he said. "Never doubt that for an instant. But it's your responsibility to serve and protect it. Do your job, Miss Bishop. *Protect my city.*"

"*Glasgow isn't-*" Leah began, and realised he had hung up.

She sat there for a moment, collecting her thoughts. She looked at Dorian, who questioned her with his eyes.

"He said something about Dylan," she told her partner. "He also confessed to the murders."

Dorian smiled without humour.

"Not that we will be able to use the confession," he said.

"No, but he says that we're missing something," she said. "I think he's trying to tell me that he didn't kill one of the Guardians, or the Attendant that Tearlach found."

"What? He killed the other supernaturals."

"Yes. But he seems to think there's something more going on."

"Perhaps," Dorian said. "But we still don't know exactly how he was able to use the pendant to kill the Fae."

"The tear pendant," Leah said. "Is there a way it can be charmed, to cause something like fatal heartbreak in people? Sebastian has magic, remember?"

Dorian stared at her, stunned.

"Why, yes," he said. "There is that possibility. He could put his charm on it but..."

Leah knew folklore too well.

"Only if he used his own tears," she said.

Dorian nodded.

"How would he know to do that?" he asked. "It's selkie magic."

"He was best friends with Magnus," said Leah, "maybe he found out. Or maybe he guessed? He was an archaeologist, after all, and might know the lore."

Dorian considered the implications of this possibility. It seemed to fit everything they knew. It wouldn't even be special magic. Nothing else would be needed but Sebastian's own tears, at the time of his wife's murder, and he would have been able to spin his own power from those atoms of starlight and pain.

"The selk live in an infinite loop of suffering," said Dorian. "It's in our nature. He would have had to trap his tears at the moment his wife died, but he would need to have some kind of iron will to be able to do that, to leave her body long enough to use the tear pendant that way."

"Maybe he found the necklace with her body," said Leah. "Magnus probably had no use for it. Or maybe Hazel got a hold of it during the struggle."

Dorian removed a white glove. He put his bare hand onto the pendant, and concentrated.

"Dorian, I don't think that's a good idea-" Leah began, but Dorian waved her words away.

The magic calls to him.

Years pile upon years like sheaves in old books, so much forgotten, so much lost.

Pressed between each page, a dead flower, is a memory.

The selkie, with his healing magic, brings the sun again, and revives the bloom.

He sees Sebastian heaving with sobs, retching on the parquet floor of the kitchen. Dorian feels the anger coursing like liquid steel through Sebastian's veins as if it were his own, giving him the strength to capture his own tears. He holds a vial and his eyes blaze as he counts the droplets. He opens the tear pendant and pours them in, mixing with Hazel's false tears stolen by Magnus.

The pendant begins to sparkle, blue and green, and a heartbeat of dark blood red spreads through it, colouring it deep and cold. Sebastian watches in utter horror and disbelief, and then puts the necklace on. He steps over Hazel's body, and crouches down beside her.

"Goodbye, my love," he whispers. "Dear God, please let her forgive me. I will find your revenge, my wife, my heart. I go to save us all."

He kisses the tear pendant, and then makes his escape, going in the opposite direction of Magnus. Dorian feels the pain, the horror, the agony of leaving his wife's body in order to pursue justice. Sebastian does not realise that the magic of the pendant has already begun to work; within him, a magic is born of fire and blood.

Dorian returned to the present, as the stolen memory faded. Leah was looking across the table at him, puzzled and more than a bit concerned.

"The tears inside were both hers and his," Dorian explained. "That would make it more powerful. Intensely so. There are very few creatures that would not be affected."

"Like Milo, and Desdemona," Leah agreed. "It also seems that it's a general power he has now, if he's in close enough proximity, given our reactions when the selk attacked him at the statue of St. George. If he became a monster due to Hazel's murder, then the necklace must contain some very powerful magic. The selk would be the ultimate victims, since heartbreak is such a central aspect of their lives. It makes sense, too, because Hazel was murdered by one of them. Sebastian must have sought out other Fae who had experienced heartbreak and somehow forced them to hold the pendant. If he could get all the selk in one place, he would be able to destroy them all with his magic. Just like Milo said, a smart bomb against a sword."

"He worked with us, at Caledonia," said Dorian. "After all, who wouldn't trust Geoffrey? He seemed so pure, so innocent."

Leah bowed her head.

"I certainly did," she said.

"Don't think you were wrong to do so," said Dorian. "Geoffrey was a good man, and so was Sebastian, once upon a time. I saw what happened. He made a choice, out of violence, from grief and pain. Before that, he was the man that Geoffrey is. You were right to trust him."

"Except that man became a killer," Leah pointed out, "despite his kindness."

"Or because of it," said Dorian, shaking his head sadly. "All those Fae, trapped in their memories."

Leah said nothing.

"Do you remember when I said that you had weapons?" Dorian asked, and she nodded. "You are stronger than you think, Leah Bishop. There is a medical term for your heart giving out because of loss and grief."

"Takutsubo cardiomyopathy," said Leah. "I remember reading about it."

"Yes," he said. "The faeries Sebastian killed, they died of a broken heart. *And you didn't.*"

Dorian lifted the pendant in his hand, gazing at the water trapped in the tiny tear-shape.

Leah watched in surprise as Dorian dropped the pendant on the floor, and crushed the glass beneath the heel of his boot.

***

The following day, as Leah walked with Dorian along the pathways of Kelvingrove Park, surrounded by the green and lush foliage of late summer, she thought perhaps she should be thanking Adam for what he had done. If he hadn't broken her heart, she'd have never taken this job.

She wouldn't have met Dorian.

Leah truly grasped that it was his loss, now. She thought of the life she would have had, if she had stayed. Stagnant, in the same town, until... what? A mortgage, children, retirement, death. And it wouldn't have been a bad life. But now? Compared to this?

She wouldn't go back to it for anything. She had changed.

"Dorian," she announced. "I have decided to stay. Here, in Glasgow, at Caledonia Interpol."

Dorian regarded her, one elegant, arched eyebrow raised above a beautiful, well-formed eye. Hundreds of centuries behind his ancient gaze, a Victorian anomaly on the mean streets of Glasgow.

He adjusted his gloves.

"Was that ever in question?" he asked.

She stared at him for a moment, and he smiled. Leah grinned back.

"What would you say to a whisky?" she asked.

"That depends. Are you buying?" he replied.

"Of course," she said.

"Single malt?"

"Only the best."

"*Slàinte,*" he replied. "I know this great little pub..."

***

Later, in the hotel, she made herself a cup of tea and looked out the window at the rain. She found it comforting now. The rain and the city.

"I haven't thought about Adam for a week," she had told Dorian, at the pub.

"You're thinking about him now," he pointed out, grinning.

She rolled her eyes.

"Yes, but..."

"The spell is broken."

She carried her mug from the window, over to the small sofa beside her bed.

"What are your weapons, Leah Bishop?"

She smiled, and pulled out her manual. She smoothed the white, clean page with the flat of her palm, and pressed the pencil down.

I am human.
My heart is my own.
I am not swayed by tradition, nor bound by magic.
I am Leah Bishop.
I am free.

The steam rose merrily from her mug of tea, and she settled in to read the rest of the manual, as the rain of Glasgow fell against her window, droplets streaking against the grey outside. She smiled, at the rain, at the wind that buffeted the glass, at the grey skies and the dirty buildings she knew stood behind the fog.

She had come home.

My name is Detective Inspector Leah Bishop.
And I'm on the monsters' side.

The End

DYLAN'S GLOSSARY

A
Aince – once
Alane – alone
Anymair – anymore
Aw – all
Awa' – away

B
Bairn – child
Buckfast – fortified tonic wine

C
Canna/cannae – can't
Celtic – Glasgow football team (green)

D
Daein' – doing
Deid – dead
Dinna/dinnae – don't
Doesnae/disnae – doesn't

F
Fae/frae – from
Fitba – football (soccer)

G
Gae – go
Gie – give

Giein – giving
Glesga - Glasgow
Greetin'/greeting – crying
Guid – good

H
Ha' – have
Hame – home

I
Irn-Bru – Glasgow's favourite soft drink
Isnae – isn't

J
Jist – just

K
Ken – know
Kent – knew

M
Ma – my
Mair – more
Mak' – make
Masel' – myself
Maw - mum

N
Nae – no
No' - not
Numptie – idiot

P

Polis – police

R

Rangers – Glasgow football team (blue)

S

S'un – something

T

Tae – to

Tak' – take

Teuchter – derogatory word for Highlander

Tha' – that

The noo – right now

W

Wee – small

Wha – who

Wi' – with

Widjae – would you

Widnae – wouldn't

Wisnae – wasn't

Wull – will

Wut/wit/whit – what

Y

Yir – you're/your

Made in the USA
Columbia, SC
01 September 2018